Dick King-Smith served with the Grenadier Guards during the Second World War, and afterwards spent twenty years as a farmer in Gloucestershire, the county of his birth. Many of his stories are inspired by his farming experiences. Later he taught at a village primary school. His first book, *The Fox Busters*, was published in 1978. Since then he has written a great number of children's books, including *The Sheep-Pig* (winner of the Guardian Award and filmed as *Babe*), *Harry's Mad*, *Noah's Brother*, *The Hodgeheg*, *Martin's Mice*, *Ace*, *The Cuckoo Child* and *Harriet's Hare* (winner of the Children's Book Award in 1995). At the British Book Awards in 1991 he was voted Children's Author of the Year. He has three children, a large number of grandchildren and several great-grandchildren, and lives in a seventeenth-century cottage only a crow's-flight from the house where he was born.

Books by Dick King-Smith

ACE

THE CUCKOO CHILD

DAGGIE DOGFOOT

DODOS ARE FOREVER

DRAGON BOY

FIND THE WHITE HORSE

THE FOX BUSTERS

HARRY'S MAD

HOW GREEN WAS MY MOUSE

JUST BINNIE

LADY DAISY

MAGNUS POWERMOUSE

MARTIN'S MICE

THE MERMAN

THE MERRYTHOUGHT

THE MOUSE BUTCHER

NOAH'S BROTHER

PADDY'S POT OF GOLD

PRETTY POLLY

THE QUEEN'S NOSE

THE ROUNDHILL

SADDLEBOTTOM

THE SCHOOLMOUSE

THE SHEEP-PIG

THE STRAY

TREASURE TROVE

THE WATER HORSE

THE WITCH OF BLACKBERRY BOTTOM

DICK KING-SMITH

Just Binnie

Illustrated by David Frankland

PUFFIN

The extract on p. 55 is from
'Times Go by Turns' by Robert Southwell

PUFFIN BOOKS

Published by the Penguin Group
Penguin Books Ltd, 80 Strand, London WC2R 0RL, England
Penguin Group (USA), Inc., 375 Hudson Street, New York, New York 10014, USA
Penguin Books Australia Ltd, 250 Camberwell Road, Camberwell, Victoria 3124, Australia
Penguin Books Canada Ltd, 10 Alcorn Avenue, Toronto, Ontario, Canada M4V 3B2
Penguin Books India (P) Ltd, 11 Community Centre, Panchsheel Park, New Delhi – 110 017, India
Penguin Group (NZ), cnr Airborne and Rosedale Roads, Albany, Auckland 1310, New Zealand
Penguin Books (South Africa) (Pty) Ltd, 24 Sturdee Avenue, Rosebank 2196, South Africa

Penguin Books Ltd, Registered Offices: 80 Strand, London WC2R 0RL, England

www.penguin.com

First published in hardback in Puffin Books 2004
Published in paperback in Puffin Books 2005

004

Text copyright © Fox Busters Ltd, 2004
Illustrations copyright © David Frankland, 2004

The moral right of the author and illustrator has been asserted

Set in 14/18.5 pt Monotype Baskerville

Made and printed in England by Clays Ltd, St Ives plc

British Library Cataloguing in Publication Data
A CIP catalogue record for this book is available from the British Library

ISBN 0–141–31620–9

www.greenpenguin.co.uk

MIX
Paper from
responsible sources
FSC
www.fsc.org   FSC® C018179

Penguin Books is committed to a sustainable
future for our business, our readers and our planet.
This book is made from Forest Stewardship
Council™ certified paper.

1

When the news came, in April 1912, Binnie Bone was out on the croquet lawn, playing a game with the two elder Bone boys, her brothers Alec and Charles. She had just hit a really splendid shot, knocking Alec's ball out of the way and getting her ball through the hoop, when Nanny Watts came out through the French windows and called her name.

Nanny Watts had been nursemaid to all six Bone children in turn – the three croquet players, their sister Dodie, their brother Edward, and now the youngest of them all, Fifi. To Watty, as they all called her, the Bones were her family.

Binnie leaned her croquet mallet against a hoop, saying to Alec and Charles, 'Shan't be a minute,' and calling, 'Coming, Watty!' as she crossed the lawn.

'Oh Binnie!' said Nanny Watts in a choky voice. 'Oh my dearest girl!'

Her eyes, Binnie could see once she was close enough, were brimming with tears and her lower lip trembled.

'Whatever's the matter, Watty?' she asked. 'Whatever has happened?'

'Your mother and father . . .' Nanny Watts began and then could go no further.

'What about Mother and Father?' Binnie asked. Nothing bad can possibly have happened to them, she thought. They're on a luxury cruise to America on the maiden voyage of the liner *Titanic*, the most splendid ship ever built.

Nanny Watts blew her nose and wiped her eyes and said shakily, 'Better call Alec and Charles,' and when the boys came over, she told them all that there had just been a telephone call from the steamship company to say that the *Titanic* had sunk.

'Sunk?' said Alec. 'She's unsinkable! They said so.'

'It seems she hit an iceberg, near Newfoundland,' said Nanny Watts, 'and she went down.'

She blew her nose again, and then went on, 'There were very few survivors, the company said. More than fifteen hundred people lost their lives. They're telephoning the next of kin of all the passengers.'

'To say if they survived or not?' said Charles.

'Yes.'

Binnie felt a chill of horror as she thought of all those poor people in an icy sea. She took a deep breath.

'And Mother and Father did not?' she said.

'Oh my poor darlings!' cried Nanny Watts, and now she broke down and wept noisily.

'We must tell the others,' said Binnie. She

did not cry, for already she was bracing herself for what she now realized was to be her future role.

At seventeen, she was the eldest of the six Bone children. Alec was one year younger, Charles two. Of the other three, Dodie was thirteen, Edward eleven, and Fifi (the Afterthought, her parents called her) was five.

Once these last three had been found and fetched from whatever they had been doing in the depths of the big old square Georgian house in which the family lived, Binnie led the way to the two long wooden benches that flanked one end of the croquet lawn.

'Sit down, all of you, please,' she said, and when they had done so (the Afterthought plumping herself on Watty's lap), she looked at them all and thought, *I hope I shall never have to do anything as hard as this again, however long I live.*

'Listen,' she said. 'Watty's just had a telephone call – Alec and Charles know about it – with news about Mother and Father.'

'Have they got to America?' Dodie asked.

'No.'

'Why not?' asked Edward.

'Because their ship – the *Titanic* – hit an iceberg.'

'What's an iceberg?' asked Fifi.

'It's a big lump of ice, darling,' said Nanny Watts.

'They'll be cold, Mother and Father will,' said Fifi.

'Do you mean,' asked Dodie, 'that the ship sank?'

'Yes,' said Binnie.

Edward, who was of a serious nature, frowned and said, 'That's why ships carry lifeboats, so that people can get in them if a ship sinks. Mother and Father will be in a lifeboat, I expect.'

'No, Edward,' said Binnie. 'They won't. They aren't.'

'Where are they, then?' asked Fifi.

Binnie looked along the faces of the six people sitting on the benches – Watty's tear-stained, Alec's and Charles's tight-lipped, Dodie's crumbling, Edward's puzzled, Fifi's round features blank and uncomprehending.

Please, God, give me strength, prayed Binnie, and

5

in answer to the Afterthought's question, she said, 'They have gone to Heaven.'

'To be with the angels?' asked Fifi.

'That's right.'

'They'll have wings then, won't they?'

'Come, Fifi darling,' said Nanny Watts and she carried the child away into the house.

'Are you saying,' said Edward slowly to Binnie, 'that they have been drowned?'

'Yes,' said Binnie, and Alec and Charles nodded, and Dodie whispered, 'Oh no!'

'Then,' said Edward, 'who will look after us?'

Binnie took a deep breath.

'I will,' she said.

2

The children's father, George Bone, had been a big man, big-hearted as well as big in body. In early middle age he still looked like the rugby player he had been as a young man. Yet he was a very gentle person, the opposite of his own father who had been – still was – very strict indeed.

In his mid-twenties George met a girl a year or so younger than himself, a girl with whom he fell instantly in love. Her name was Henrietta Fea. She was a pretty girl, small in build and looking even smaller beside George, with straight dark hair in contrast to his fairness.

The marriage was a happy one, becoming, if possible, even happier as each of the six children made his or her appearance.

'Henny,' said George Bone to his wife in the autumn of 1911, 'do you realize that before long we shall have been married for twenty years?'

Henrietta took down a copy of *Pears Cyclopaedia* from a bookshelf and found 'Wedding Anniversaries'.

'That will be our china anniversary,' she said.

'Well, let's celebrate it in a very special way,' said George.

'By going to China?'

'No, to America. There's this new ocean liner that's going to have her maiden voyage next April. Why don't I telephone the shipping company and book us a cabin? How would you like that, Henny darling?'

'Oh George,' said Henrietta, 'I think I should love it. But what about the children?'

8

'Well, Watty's here, and Binnie is pretty responsible. And we shan't be away all that long.'

'I suppose not,' said Henrietta. 'But I've never been to sea before. I might be a bit nervous.'

'Nervous? Of what?'

Henrietta giggled.

'Oh, I don't know,' she said. 'The ship might sink. They do sometimes.'

'Not this one,' said George. 'She is unsinkable.'

'Oh good!' said Henrietta.

'And I should think,' said George, 'that both lots of grandparents would probably offer to have the children whilst we're away. Three to my parents, three to yours perhaps.'

George Bone's parents and those of his wife could hardly have been less alike.

George's father, General Hereward Bone, had fought in the first Boer War, and he still looked and behaved like a soldier. Tall, upright, with a heavy moustache, Grandfather Bone was very strict with his children, and George had been brought up to obey orders without question. As, too, had both his brothers, each of whom had escaped from the General's heavy hand by

9

getting as far away from it as possible, once they were old enough. One had gone to Canada, the other to Australia.

Perhaps it was because of his father's attitude that George had grown up to be so gentle and easy-going, careful that none of his own children should be ordered about as he had been.

Granny Bone, the General's wife, had never challenged her husband's authority in any way. Patience was her name and she must have had a deal of it. She was a quiet and unassuming person, and George and Henrietta's children were very much fonder of her than they were of the General.

Henrietta's mother and father were totally different kinds of people from George's parents and indeed, again, from one another.

Granny Fea was, it must be said, a silly woman. She meant well but she had a remarkable knack of saying and doing foolish things, apparently amusing herself while maddening almost everyone else.

Strangely, she did not seem to annoy her husband, but this was because nothing annoyed

Reggie Fea, the most easy-going of men. A small-ish, round, comfortable person, he was above all else lazy. He was the perfect husband for the prattling empty-headed Felicity Fea because he could never be bothered to listen to anything she said. A wealthy man, he had never worked for a living.

General Bone could not stand Reggie Fea, despising his idleness and apparent lack of back-bone. Reggie did not particularly dislike the General – that would have demanded too much effort – but instead saw him as a figure of fun. He could imitate Grandfather Bone's rasping voice to perfection, though he never did it in front of the grandchildren. He liked though to try it out now and again on his wife, who would always burst out laughing and say, 'Why, Reggie, you sound just like Hereward Bone!'

'Really? Well, well! Ha, ha!' Reggie would say, settling back into the comfort of his armchair before the fire.

The Bone children loved Grandpa Reggie, who never ordered them about as Grandfather Bone did. It would have been too much effort.

They didn't mind Granny Fea but each secretly preferred Granny Bone.

Different as all the four grandparents were – Hereward the strict soldier and his mousy wife, lazy Reggie and his foolish Felicity – all were equally affected by the telephone call from their eldest grandchild that came to each of their houses on that quiet, sunny April evening in 1912.

3

The lifestyles of George Bone and his wife and of both their sets of parents were very similar. Each couple lived in the same sort of big, comfortable country house, houses that had living-in servants and large grounds looked after by gardeners. Moreover, they all lived fairly close to one another, in that part of southern England where the three counties of Gloucestershire,

Wiltshire and Somerset come together. The nearest city for all of them was Bath, and it was here indeed that George and Henrietta had first met, at a dance in the Pump Room.

Their house was in Somerset, the Feas' in Wiltshire, while the General's somewhat barrack-like mansion stood in Gloucestershire.

It was the General to whom Binnie first telephoned, and it was Granny Bone who took the call, at her husband's command.

'Answer the thing, can't you, Patience?' the General shouted. 'I'm busy.'

Had he been near enough, he would have heard his wife saying 'Hello?' and then 'Hello, Binnie dear!' and then, after a long pause, 'Oh no!'

At the Feas' Elizabethan manor house in Wiltshire, it was Grandpa Reggie who took Binnie's call. The telephone stood on a table close beside his armchair, to make the answering of it as little trouble as possible to him.

Granny Fea came into the room as he was replacing the receiver, and saw that he was deathly pale.

'Why, Reggie,' she said with her high, nervous laugh. 'You look as though you've seen a ghost!'

Once they had begun to take in Binnie's dreadful news, the grandparents telephoned one another, and it was decided (by the General) that all four would travel to George's house as early as possible next day, and it was suggested (by Reggie Fea) that they should all travel in his motorcar. Grandfather Bone did not own a car and, left to himself, would have ridden there on horseback, leaving his wife to make her way as she might. Grandpa Reggie, bestirring himself for once in his life, gave orders for his chauffeur to make ready the Rolls-Royce Silver Ghost in which, when he absolutely had to, he travelled. He himself had never learned to drive it – too much trouble.

The following morning the six Bone children and Nanny Watts all stood waiting at the foot of the flight of stone steps that led up to the front door of the square Georgian house that had been, for almost twenty years, the home of George and Henrietta. It was called Combe Brindle House, and up its drive now swept Grandpa Reggie's Rolls-Royce.

*

15

When all were settled comfortably in the drawing-room, and the parlourmaid had brought coffee and biscuits, and Nanny Watts had tactfully withdrawn to her own quarters, Grandfather Bone called the meeting to order. Or that is how an outsider might have seen it, as the General rose to his feet, pulling at that heavy moustache, and stared round at the assembled company: his wife sitting still and quiet, Granny Fea smiling rather foolishly, Grandpa Reggie – at ease in the most comfortable of the chairs – looking intently at the children.

The General cleared his throat.

'Be good enough to listen to me, all of you,' he said. 'Obviously this is a terrible occasion for all of us, and equally obviously we must lose no time in making arrangements for the future.'

He turned to Binnie.

'As the eldest of the children,' he said to her, 'you will understand, my dear, that in the absence of your parents it is the duty of your grandparents to look after you.'

He turned to face Reggie Fea.

'You would agree with that, Fea?' he said.

'Undoubtedly,' replied Grandpa Reggie, 'and equally without doubt, General, you will have already come up with a plan of action.'

'Indeed,' said the General. 'Obviously six children cannot continue to live here at Combe Brindle House without adult supervision,' and he looked towards the two grandmothers, who nodded, one thoughtfully, one vacantly.

'Excuse me, sir,' said Alec, 'but we do have an adult in the house.'

'Don't interrupt, boy,' said the General. 'I'm not talking of servants.'

'Nor am I, sir,' said Alec. 'I mean Nanny Watts.'

'And Watty's not a servant,' put in Dodie. 'She's our friend.'

Fifi, who had been playing with a favourite old Dutch doll and paying no attention to the General's speech, now said loudly, 'Watty's *my* friend.'

'Does she understand', said Grandpa Reggie to Binnie, 'what has happened to her mother and father?'

'Mother and Father', said Fifi, 'are on an

17

iceberg,' at which Granny Fea tittered and Binnie said quietly to her youngest sister, 'Run and find Watty, Fifi, and perhaps she'll take you for a walk in the garden.'

'I'm sorry,' she said to the four grandparents when the child had gone. 'She's a bit too young to take it in.'

'Now,' said the General, frowning, 'perhaps you will allow me to finish what I was saying.'

'As quickly as you can,' said Reggie Fea under his breath, 'you pompous old windbag.'

'What I suggest, Fea,' said the General, 'is that George's children be divided between us, so that each is responsible for three of them. What do you say to that?'

Slowly Reggie Fea heaved his small tubby body out of his chair. He stood, looking, as ever, as if he had slept in his comfortably crumpled clothes, and gazed up at the other grandfather.

'On a point of order, General,' he said, smiling, 'I would remind you that George's children, as you put it, are also Henrietta's children.'

'Of course, of course,' huffed the General.

'Secondly, if three of our grandchildren are to

come and live in my house and three in yours, how are we to decide who goes where? Do we toss for them?'

'No, no,' said Grandfather Bone irritably. 'The division is perfectly simple. I have the three boys, you have the three girls.'

There was a silence, during which Alec, Charles and Edward considered the thought of life at Mafeking Towers under the command of the General (fond as they were of his wife), while Binnie and Dodie wondered how they and the Afterthought would cope with living at Littledown Manor with Grandpa Reggie and feather-brained Granny Fea.

'Well?' said the General to the company at large.

'Ask them,' said Grandpa Reggie. 'Ask Binnie – she's the eldest.'

'Well, Binnie?' said the General.

Binnie stood up. *This is a crucial moment,* she said to herself. *I mustn't let Grandfather split the family up like this. Just because he's been used to ordering soldiers about doesn't mean he can tell me what's to be done. I've got to make the decisions.*

'We'll see, Grandfather,' she said.

'"We'll see"? What do you mean by that?'

Binnie Bone, dark-haired like her mother and tall as her father had been, looked at her father's father, white-haired now but straight-backed still, dressed in his customary mustard-coloured tweed suit, with his regimental tie knotted precisely beneath a high stiff collar and his brown boots polished to a gleaming shine. Her head tilted a little, her grey eyes looked unflinchingly into the General's hot brown ones.

'I mean, Grandfather,' she said, 'that I will consider the plan that you have suggested, and that, between the six of us, we will decide what is to be done.'

4

'Gosh, Bin!' said Alec. 'You really stood up to Grandfather B. I thought the old chap was going to explode!'

'I don't like to be bullied,' said Binnie.

It was now the afternoon of the grandparents' visit, the Silver Ghost had vanished down the drive of Combe Brindle House, and the two eldest Bone children were playing a game of croquet on the lawn.

The General's reaction to Binnie's quiet statement of intent had indeed been a very angry one. That a child, one of his own grandchildren at that, should calmly say that *she* would decide what was to be done was nothing less than mutiny in the ranks.

For a while he had shouted and blustered, insisting that Binnie should do as she was told, while Grandpa Reggie put a hand over his face to hide a smile.

But Binnie merely repeated that she and the other children would make the decisions, until at last the General, sensing defeat, was forced into a tactical withdrawal.

'I refuse to listen to any more of this nonsense from this slip of a girl,' he growled. 'I shall stay here no longer. Patience, get your hat and coat.'

'Had I better get mine too, Reggie?' asked Granny Fea.

'We can hardly let the General march back to Mafeking Towers,' replied her husband, and to Alec he said, 'Perhaps you would tell my chauffeur to bring the Rolls round to the front door.'

*

After their game, Binnie and Alec sat for a moment on the bench at the end of the croquet lawn.

'Do you really think you can do it, Bin?' Alec said.

'Do what?'

'Well, take Mother and Father's place, so that we can stay on here.'

'I hope so,' Binnie said. 'With your help. Grandfather B's plan may have been well meant, but the last thing I want is for us to be split up like that.'

'Hear, hear!' said Alec. 'You girls might have been all right with Grandpa Reggie, but for me and Charles and Edward, it'd have been just like joining the Army, I should think.'

They sat in the April sunshine for a little while without speaking, and then Binnie said, 'When does term start?'

Alec and Charles were at Marlborough College in Wiltshire, while Edward was at a preparatory school in the Cotswolds. This meant three lots of boarding-school fees to be met.

As was usual at that time the girls were taught

at home. Their governess was a retired school-teacher who lived in the village and came up to Combe Brindle House each weekday morning.

'May the fifth for Charles and me,' Alec said. 'Not sure about Edward – probably the same date. But Bin, where's the money going to come from, for school fees?'

'From Father's estate, I imagine,' Binnie replied. 'Grandpa Reggie says that he would certainly have made a will and that we'll just have to wait for probate.'

'What's that mean?'

'Proving that the will is correct in every way.'

'That might take ages, mightn't it?' asked Alec.

'Perhaps,' said Binnie, 'especially as I suppose that Mother and Father are only presumed dead.'

'So how do we manage in the meantime?'

'We shall need help. It isn't just the school fees – there's the housekeeping expenses and clothes to be bought and the servants to be paid and goodness knows what else.'

'But how . . .?' began Alec.

'Hang on,' said Binnie. 'Here's Watty coming with Fifi.'

*

Lying in bed that night, Binnie thought, *We'll have to have help from the grandparents for the time being. I shouldn't think that Grandfather B would lift a finger after what I said, but perhaps Grandpa Reggie might.*

For a long time she could not get to sleep and when at last she did, her dreams were full of her parents. She woke next morning heavy-hearted. How could she possibly take their place and be head of the family? Not only would she have to make all the decisions usually made by her father, but she would have to run the house as her mother had done. Among other things, this meant planning all the meals and the servants' work, keeping the household accounts, and making sure everything ran smoothly in the big house. And of course, most importantly, she would have to be mother and father to her brothers and sisters.

She got out of bed and knelt at the side of it, head bent, palms together, as Watty had taught her to do when she was little.

'Please God,' she said softly, 'help me to look after my brothers and sisters. Amen.'

She dressed and went downstairs. As usual the

letters had been picked up off the mat inside the front door and placed neatly on a small table in the hall. She sieved through them but there seemed nothing to comfort her. In fact she felt worse when she saw there were several letters for her father that were obviously bills.

But later in the day, when the afternoon post was delivered, there was just a single letter, addressed to 'Miss Bone', the proper title for an eldest girl, in the familiar scrawly handwriting of Grandpa Reggie.

Binnie opened it.

Littledown Manor
April 18th 1912.

My dear Binnie,

We are just arrived home, having deposited the General and Mrs General at Mafeking Towers, and I write immediately to catch the evening post – to thank you for your hospitality and to congratulate you on your bravery in confronting your other grandfather.

Be assured, dear Binnie, that the General thought he was acting in your best interests and those of the other children in advancing his scheme for looking after you all.

Due to your gallant intervention (you deserve a VC – Very Courageous) I was spared the effort – had I summoned up the nerve to do so – of disagreeing with him.

I think it most important that the six of you should continue to live at Combe Brindle House, your own home, and I have no doubt that in due course monies from your father's estate will enable you to do so. However, these things take time, and I want you to know that I will meet any and every expense until such time as you may know your position more clearly.

Your affectionate grandfather,

Reginald Fea

'Thank you, thank you, God!' said Binnie softly.

5

A stranger, meeting the six Bone children, would have been in no doubt that they were brothers and sisters. There were differences in colouring (Alec and Charles were fair-haired, the rest dark) and in build (Dodie was on the tubby side, Edward slighter than his brothers), but their faces were very alike.

Now that their parents were gone, there was

probably no one who knew their various characters as well as Nanny Watts, who had played (and was still playing in the case of Fifi) such an important part in their upbringing.

Had anyone asked her to describe each child in a few words, she might well have said something like this:

'Binnie – reliable, responsible, old for her years.

'Alec – a sensible sort of boy but inclined to be lazy, a bit of a dreamer.

'Charles – happy-go-lucky, full of energy, mad about cricket and also machinery – cars, for example, and those newfangled aeroplanes.

'Dodie – quiet, a bit shy, loves animals.

'Edward – serious, interested in learning, a bit of a loner.

'Fifi,' Watty might have said finally, 'is my favourite, truth to tell, partly of course because she's the youngest of the six and so the one that still needs me most, especially now that she is motherless. Mind you, she's as stubborn as a mule.'

Mulish the Afterthought certainly was in the days that followed. Perhaps because she sensed, even though not fully understanding, the tragedy that had happened, she became for a while an awkward little madam, often refusing to do as Nanny Watts said, throwing fits of temper or lapsing into sulks, and generally playing the spoiled child.

Even her beloved Dutch doll, Florence, was denied her usual affection, and indeed was, on occasion, dragged around by her hair, her wooden feet trailing forlornly along the ground.

'Poor Florence!' Watty would say. 'Be nice to her, Fifi darling, can't you?' But the child's face was as expressionless as the doll's.

Edward had always been different in character from his older brothers. There were only twenty months between Alec and Charles, while Edward was almost four years younger, and until Fifi's arrival, he had been the baby of the family.

He was a serious-minded boy who normally seemed quite happy with his own company, especially at home. Going back to school at the start of a new term was for him an ordeal, when for the first few days at any rate he shed many quiet tears in the darkness of the dormitory. Now he was trying hard to come to grips with the knowledge that he would never see his father and mother again. *Why has this awful thing happened?* Edward thought. *How am I going to be able to bear it?*

Above his bed hung a picture of Jesus, the Son of God, his kindly bearded face looking lovingly down on a motley crowd of children of many nations sitting at his feet.

How could God let such a thing happen to me? said Edward to himself.

Dodie sought comfort from her pets. All the Bone children liked animals, and there had always been dogs and cats sharing their home. But from an early age Dodie had been fascinated by rabbits and guinea pigs, and once she was old enough to care for them properly, had been allowed to keep both. In the nature of things, the rabbits and guinea pigs soon grew in number. They were kept in hutches in an old shed, where Dodie spent a lot of time looking after them and talking to them. Often, when there were visitors to Combe Brindle House, she would retire to her shed.

Now she sought to comfort herself by telling her animals what had happened. The rabbits listened in silence, their ears pricked, but the guinea pigs commented loudly on the news with much squeaking and chattering. Dodie found this comforting.

Charles was just as upset as the rest of the children, but tried hard to put it out of his mind by concentrating his thoughts on the forthcoming cricket season. In the next term at Marlborough, he would move from a Junior to a Senior House, and all his daydreams were of success to come on the cricket pitch.

Hanging above his bed was another kindly bearded face, that of W. G. Grace, scorer of nearly 55,000 runs including 126 centuries, and now sixty-four years old. *If I practise really hard*, said Charles to himself, *I might be selected for my House First Eleven one day and then, perhaps, for the school.*

STYLISH OPENING BATSMAN SCORES MAIDEN CENTURY FOR MARLBOROUGH – he could just see the headline.

In the kitchen gardens there was a fruit-pen whose netting protected the strawberries and raspberries within from raiding birds. Making use of one side of this pen and of a straight path that led towards it, Charles persuaded Alec to bowl to him as often as he could, in these makeshift 'nets'. If Alec wasn't around then Whittle the gardener would bowl, as Charles tried to perfect his batting and especially that towering 'six' that would one day win the match but at the moment simply soared clean out of the kitchen gardens.

Unlike Charles, Alec's interest in cricket was limited. He bowled to his brother when he could be bothered, but above all else he was a book-worm, never happier than when he had his nose in a story, preferably an adventure story. Alec was the kind of person who would rather read about people dicing with death than have to do so him-self. But now, of course, death was very much on his mind, and he asked himself whether it was right that Binnie should be, apparently, setting herself up as head of this family of orphans. He, Alec, was the eldest boy and Binnie was only a girl, after all. *But maybe*, he thought, *she'll do it better than I would.*

Binnie herself had been following the same

line of thinking: *Men were always the heads of families, and even though Alec was still only a boy of sixteen, shouldn't he be the one to make the decisions?*

But then in many ways, she thought, *he's quite a young sixteen, while I — if I wasn't grown up before — I certainly am now. It's my fault, if fault there is, for saying that I'd look after them all.*

There's going to be such a lot to do, such a lot of things to think about, practical matters like food and clothes and the boys' schooling. But I suppose the most important thing that I have to aim for is that the six of us shall be happy.

Learning to live our lives without Mother and Father is going to be hard, but what's happened has happened. The most I can hope for is the happiness of the six of us, and what's more, I ought to be leading by example.

Binnie stood before the tall mirror in her bedroom and looked at her face.

'Better start practising,' she said, and she managed a rueful grin.

6

'You came to live here before I was born, didn't you, Watty?' Binnie said.

They were sitting in Nanny Watts's little living-room at the top of the house. Late April it might be but the coal fire burning in the grate was welcome that evening. Binnie sat at one side of it and Watty on the other.

As she looked at Watty – short, plump and comfortable-looking, wire-rimmed spectacles perched on her snub nose, her greying hair done in the usual neat bun – Binnie thought she seemed never to have changed in appearance since first she could remember.

'I came to work for your dear mother and father,' Nanny Watts replied, 'a couple of months before you were born, Binnie, love.'

'So you've been with us for just about eighteen years?'

'Yes, I was thirty-two when I came to Combe Brindle House.'

'So this year you'll be fifty! You don't look it, Watty,' Binnie said.

'I feel it, Binnie. Oh, how I miss them!' Watty said and she pulled a handkerchief from the pocket of her apron and dabbed at her eyes.

'So do we all,' said Binnie.

I must try to cheer her up, she thought. *I know!* She did a quick bit of mental arithmetic.

'So,' she said, 'you were born in . . . 1862.'

'That's right. 26 May 1862.'

'Well, on 26 May 1912,' Binnie said, 'you are going to have a really special birthday party, I promise you. Would you like that?'

'Oh Binnie,' said Nanny Watts, 'I don't know. I don't think I'm in much of a party mood, as things are.'

'I don't think any of us are at the moment,' Binnie said, 'but life's got to go on. Mother and Father wouldn't want us all to be miserable forever, and they would certainly have wanted to celebrate your fiftieth birthday if they'd been here. So you're going to have a party, Watty, like it or not. Is that understood? Don't forget, I'm the head of this family now, or at any rate I'm trying to be.'

She rose from her chair, pulled Watty to her feet, and smiled down at her.

'So you must do as you're told,' she said.

Going back along the passage towards the stairs, Binnie had to pass the door of the night-nursery, next door to Watty's room. Each of the Bone children had slept there in their turn. The door was ajar and Binnie peeped in to see, by the glow of a night-light, Fifi sleeping quietly.

She tiptoed to the bedside and bent and kissed the dark mop of the Afterthought's curly hair.

The child did not stir, but in her sleep spoke one word.

'Mama?' said Fifi.

Binnie waited awhile, but her youngest sister's breathing was steady and regular and she made no further sound.

I know now what they mean, thought Binnie as she made her way downstairs, *when they talk of people being heartbroken. But I can't allow my heart to be broken – I mustn't. There's too much to be done.*

She passed the door of the billiard-room, where Alec and Charles were playing a game of snooker, and heard the click of the billiard balls and the boys' voices and then a sudden burst of laughter at something or other.

Laugh away, boys, she said to herself. *We've all got to learn to laugh again.*

Binnie went on and turned into the smoking-room. It was called that, the children had always supposed, because it was the room where Father sat to smoke his pipe, in his own big leather armchair at the side of the broad open fireplace. The drawing-room next door was much larger and more elegant, but the smoking-room was, above all, cosy. Now the leather armchair was unoccupied, but a good log fire burned in the grate, and Edward sat at a gate-legged table before it, playing Patience.

Watching him as he laid out the cards, Binnie thought how young and vulnerable he looked. She put a hand on his shoulder.

'Are you all right, Teddy?' she asked.

For a moment her youngest brother did not answer, but then he said in a choky voice, 'No, I'm not, Bin,' and began to cry.

Binnie knelt beside his chair and put her arms round him.

'What is it, old chap?' she said. 'Tell me.'

For a while Edward could not reply, but then he wiped his eyes and sniffed and gulped and said, 'It's school. I don't want to go back to school. Must I?'

Binnie sighed. *Poor fellow*, she thought, *he's only just eleven*.

'Yes, Teddy dear,' she replied. 'I think you must.'

'But *they* won't come and see me there,' he said miserably. '*They* won't come to take me out on a

Sunday. There won't be any letters ever again. It'll be awful.'

'You've got to be brave,' Binnie said. 'There's no other way. We'll all come and see you, probably we'll come in Grandpa Reggie's car. We'll take you out on Sundays and we'll write to you.'

She got up and moved across to the big leather armchair and patted its seat.

'Come and sit here a minute,' she said.

'But that's Father's chair,' said Edward.

'And Father would want you to be brave and not make a fuss about going back to school. Come and sit here for a moment. It might help.'

Edward looked very small, sitting in that deep seat. On a table beside the armchair stood George Bone's pipe-rack with its array of pipes and his tobacco jar. *There was still*, Binnie thought, *a faint aroma of tobacco in the air.*

'Well, Teddy?' she said.

'Sorry,' he said. 'I'll be all right now,' and he heaved himself out of the leather armchair and went back to his game of Patience.

Next minute Dodie came into the smoking-room.

'Oh Bin,' she said. 'Can you help me?'

'Of course,' replied Binnie. 'What do you want?'

'Can you come down to my shed, please?' Dodie said. 'It'll be dark soon and then I shan't be able to do it till tomorrow.'

'Do what?'

'Measure Marjorie.'

Marjorie was one of Dodie's guinea pigs, and measuring, Binnie knew, was an important part of Dodie's pet-keeping routine. The sows – the female guinea pigs – regularly became pregnant, and Dodie liked to be properly prepared for new arrivals.

To this end she would measure each sow round its middle, and record the results in a carefully kept notebook. When the waistline of any individual showed regular and satisfactory increase, Dodie then resorted to the final test to determine how near each was to giving birth.

This consisted of putting the sow's head into the opening of a short length of earthenware drainpipe, and then encouraging the expectant mother to go through this tunnel. If it could not, if it was too fat, then Dodie would move the animal into a special roomy hutch which she called the Labour Ward.

This last routine was simple – either the sow could go through the drainpipe or it couldn't – but measuring was more easily done by two people, one to hold the guinea pig, one to slip the tape-measure round its belly.

So now Binnie went down with Dodie to her shed, and held the pregnant Marjorie while Dodie made the measurements.

'Eleven and a half inches,' she said and then, consulting her notebook, 'She's up half an inch.'

'Time for the drainpipe?' Binnie asked.

'No, not yet. Marjorie will get a lot fatter than this,' said Dodie, and she put the sow back in its hutch.

'Thanks, Bin,' she said.

Just as she had enquired of Edward, Binnie now said, 'Are you all right, Dodie?' but this time the answer was 'Yes.'

'You're coping, are you?' said Binnie.

'Yes,' said Dodie.

She moved along the row of hutches, looking into each in turn.

'We talk about what has happened, you see,' she said. 'It helps, doesn't it, my dears?' And in answer there came quite a chorus of chunterings and chitterings.

7

When another week had passed, the newspapers printed the names of all the survivors of the *Titanic* disaster. Then it was that families throughout Great Britain finally knew that the time for miracles was past, that if the names of their loved ones were not on that list they would never see them again. They were dead and gone and there were no bodies to bury.

But we must do something, the families thought. *We must hold services of remembrance for them, to give thanks for their lives and to pray for their souls.*

Oddly, in the Bone family it was not the grand-parents who first thought this, nor uncles and aunts, and not even Binnie or Alec. It was Edward who voiced the idea, at the last break-fast of the spring holidays. Later that morning Grandpa Reggie's Silver Ghost was due to appear at Combe Brindle House, to carry first Edward to his Cotswold prep school and then the other two boys to Marlborough, for the summer term.

Now trunks and tuck-boxes were packed and waiting in the hall, plus, of course, all Charles's cricketing gear, and the six children and Nanny Watts were sitting at table, when Edward suddenly said, 'I've been thinking. Mother and Father will never be buried in the village church-yard, will they?'

Oh goodness! thought Binnie. *I hope he's not going to make himself extra-miserable, and on the day he's going back to school, what's more.*

'No, they can't be, Teddy,' she said, and Fifi remarked, as usual, that they were on an iceberg, a state of affairs with which she seemed quite happy.

'But they ought to be remembered,' said Edward.

'Of course they will be,' the others all said.

'I didn't mean that,' Edward said. 'I meant that we all ought to go to church one day and have a service, specially for them.'

'You're right, Teddy,' said Alec and Charles together, and Dodie, fat Marjorie on her lap, smiled and nodded at him, and Fifi said, 'Can I have some more porridge?'

'Of course he's right,' said Binnie. 'How stupid of me not to have made plans for it. I'll go down to the Vicar and fix a date, Teddy. It's sure to mean that you three boys will all have to be brought back from your schools for a day, but I don't suppose you'll mind that.'

'It will be on a Sunday, I imagine?' Alec said.

'Oh yes.'

'Oh good,' said Charles. 'There'll be no cricket on Sundays.'

When the younger ones had left the table and only Nanny Watts and Binnie were still sitting at it, Watty said, 'Don't you think that perhaps your grandfathers ought to be arranging any service of remembrance, one for his son, one for his daughter?'

'Grandfather Bone, perhaps,' Binnie replied. 'I don't know if Grandpa Reggie would want to be saddled with it.'

'But the General definitely would, wouldn't he?' said Watty.

'Yes,' said Binnie. 'Perhaps I should telephone him.'

Later that day, she did. The goodbyes had been said and all three boys had gone, Alec and Charles half regretful at leaving home, half excited at the thought of reunion with their friends and, in Charles's case, of a long drive in the car. He was fascinated by the Rolls-Royce and the mechanics of driving.

Edward, when he left, was pale but dry-eyed. When Binnie hugged him, she whispered in his ear those same words, 'Are you all right?' and he nodded.

Once Fifi was happily talking with her Watty and Dodie was chatting with her guinea pigs,

Binnie gave the telephone operator the number of Mafeking Towers. She had prepared in her mind what she was going to say to her grandfather, the General, but it was Granny Bone who answered, with the formula she always employed with the telephone.

'Who calls?' she asked in her soft voice.

'It's me, Granny. Binnie.'

'Binnie dear,' said Granny Bone. 'You wanted to speak with your grandfather, I dare say?'

'Yes, please, Granny.'

'He's out, dear. Can I take a message?'

So Binnie explained what it was she had in mind.

'I thought Grandfather would want to arrange it all,' she said.

'I'm sure he would, dear,' said Granny Bone, 'but I've a better idea.'

'What is that?'

'You go and make all the arrangements with your vicar – date, time, form of service, everything – and then when you've done all that, I will suggest to your grandfather that it is of course he who should organize a service of remembrance.

Then I'll suggest that he telephone your vicar, who will indicate to him what it is that you have arranged but not that it was you who arranged it, and your grandfather will think that it is all his own work. How about that for an idea, Binnie?' said her grandmother.

'Oh Granny!' said Binnie. 'How clever of you.'

'There are lots of good things in small parcels,' said Granny Bone.

Next, Binnie made a telephone call to Little-down Manor. She thought that her mother's parents would like to know from her what was being planned, and she also thought that Grandpa Reggie would be amused at the small deception that was to be practised upon the General. Indeed he was, to the extent that he put on his imitation of his fellow grandfather's harsh tones.

'Damned good idea, what?' he growled to Binnie. 'No one better qualified to run the show, doncherknow!'

Granny Fea came into the room at that moment, and when he had replaced the receiver

said, giggling, 'I do declare, Reggie, that sometimes you sound to me exactly like Hereward
Bone!'

Her telephoning done, Binnie walked down to
the Vicarage.

Robin Seymour, Vicar of St Margaret's,
Combe Brindle, was, as she had thought he would
be, only too willing to fall in with the plan that
Granny Bone had suggested, and between them
they fixed upon a Sunday afternoon in ten days'
time.

'I'll feed the date and the hour to the General,'
the Vicar said, 'and with a bit of luck he'll swal-
low it whole. The church will be packed, you
know, Binnie, I have no doubt. Your mother
and father were well loved. I am so glad that
you want this service. I was on the point of sug-
gesting such a thing myself but held back, as
I imagine you did, until the final announcement
of the names of the survivors was published. Tell
me, how are you managing?'

'As best I can.'

'Who is to cope with all that needs to be done?'

'I am, Mr Seymour,' Binnie said. She smiled.

'Perhaps you had better pray for me,' she said.

The Vicar smiled at her in return.

'I will,' he said. 'It's a funny thing, but I am a great believer in the power of prayer.'

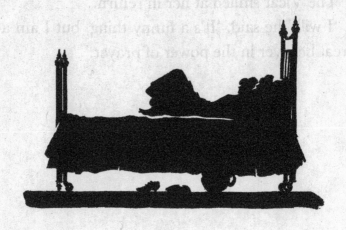

8

The Vicar was right. When the day came, St Margaret's Church was chock-full.

In one front pew sat the six Bone children, with Watty at Fifi's side. The front pew on the other side of the aisle contained the four grandparents, their father's two brothers back from abroad and their mother's two sisters. Behind were a number of other relatives, a good many friends, and a host of people from the village, so that, thanks to the Vicar's choice of more than usually cheerful hymns and a better than usual organist, the singing of the congregation was to reach record heights of volume.

There were two Lessons, one read by the General in parade-ground tones, the other, more gently, by Reggie Fea, and the Vicar gave a short talk in which, in simple but telling words, he paid tribute to the memory of George Bone and his wife Henrietta.

Binnie read a poem.

She had thought a lot about doing this, about standing up in front of a church full of people and reciting. Could she do it well enough? Suppose her nerve failed her and her throat tightened so that she could not get the words out? Should she ask Alec, as the eldest son, to do it? For she felt strongly that one of their children ought to read something in Mother and Father's memory.

'I don't want to,' Alec said. 'I'd sooner you did, Bin.'

Binnie decided to enlist the help of the Vicar.

'I can't just take part in the service without

Grandfather being told,' she said. 'Could you put it to him, Mr Seymour, please?' and later that day he reported that he had telephoned the General and suggested such a reading.

'What did he say?' Binnie asked.

'His actual words,' the Vicar said, 'if I remember rightly, were, "Well, if the girl wants to do it, I suppose she'd better. Got no use for poetry myself. Only poem I ever liked was *The Charge of the Light Brigade*."'

After a great deal of searching, Binnie found a poem which began with a reference to the sea, and which said what she felt – that happiness ends but time heals.

Now the day had come, the hour had come, the very moment when she must play her part was upon her.

As the last notes of a hymn died away and the congregation sat down again, Binnie rose to her feet and stepped out of her pew and went to stand in front of all the rows of people. She had decided not to read the poem but rather to learn it by heart – it was only six lines.

She was standing directly in front of her two

grandmothers who were sitting side by side, and now she began to speak those lines, trying hard to speak clearly and with meaning and not too fast:

'The sea of fortune doth not ever flow,
She draws her favours to the lowest ebb;
Her tide hath equal times to come and go,
Her loom doth weave the fine and coarsest web;
No joy so great but runneth to an end,
No hap so hard but may in time amend.'

As Binnie returned to her seat, Granny Fea whispered to Granny Bone, 'She looked very nice, I thought. Though I'm not sure the colour of that dress suits her.'

'Did you not listen to what she read, Felicity?' asked Granny Bone softly.

'Oh no, Patience. I don't know anything about poetry,' said Granny Fea, 'but I'm sure she read it very well.'

After the service there was an enormous tea for family and friends, and at one point the two grandfathers found themselves face to face.

'Went pretty well, Fea, don't you think?' said Hereward Bone.

'All due to your guiding hand, General,' said Reggie Fea. 'No one better qualified to run the show.'

At this point the Vicar joined them.

'Don't you agree, Vicar?' Grandpa Reggie went on.

'Agree with what?'

'That the General here organized this afternoon's service most admirably. You yourself spoke so well and movingly of course, but his choice of hymns and lessons and so forth, and his splendid idea of having our dear Binnie recite that poem was a masterstroke. All quite brilliant of him, don't you think?' said Reggie Fea, and one of his eyes closed for an instant, unseen by the General but to the Vicar an unmistakable wink.

Robin Seymour smiled.

'I quite agree,' he said. 'Especially about Binnie. Let us hope that the whole thing will have gone some way to hearten her and the other children.'

Indeed Binnie was heartened by all the nice things that people said about her parents – what a splendid couple they had been, how they would be missed. 'What can we do to help you?' people asked, and there were many kind offers of assistance in one way or another.

Even the General seemed more mellow than usual.

'You did well, my dear,' he said to Binnie. 'You read that poetry stuff very nicely. I think it all went off well, don't you?'

'I do, Grandfather,' Binnie said. 'I only hope that you and Granny will not be too tired at the end of the day.'

'Tired?' said the General. 'Good heavens, no. It's only a matter of ten miles to get home, and that pony of ours pulls the dogcart at a spanking rate.'

He cleared his throat.

'By the way, Binnie,' he said. 'I'm sorry I spoke sharply to you the other day. I was out of order.'

'That's all right, Grandfather,' Binnie said, 'and don't worry about us.'

She reached up to kiss him.

'How are you managing?' Grandpa Reggie said to her a little later.

'All right.'

'Now look. I've had a talk with my bank manager and arranged finances for you, so don't worry about the money side of things. We can sort everything out once your mother and father's wills are proved.'

'Thank you, Grandpa,' said Binnie, and bent to kiss him for he was a little shorter than her.

For a couple of hours Binnie moved about the rooms, talking to people, making sure they had enough to eat and drink, playing the hostess as she thought her mother would have expected her to do. But eventually the last sandwiches, the last cakes were eaten, all the goodbyes were said and everyone had left.

There were a couple of other motor-cars beside the Rolls, some near neighbours bicycled or walked away, and off went the General and Granny Bone and their two sons in the dogcart. The Silver Ghost ferried a number of people to the nearby railway station, before finally departing with the Fea grandparents and their two daughters. Next day, it would return to take the boys back to their schools.

The servants apart, once again Combe Brindle House contained only six children and their nanny.

By agreement, nobody bothered much with supper – they were all too full from what had been an enormous tea. In the gap before bedtime Watty was reading a story to Fifi, Edward was reading a story to himself, Dodie was feeding her rabbits and guinea pigs, and Alec and Charles were on the croquet lawn.

As for Binnie, she suddenly felt tired. It had been quite a day. She went up to her bedroom and lay upon the bed, hands behind her head, looking up at the ceiling.

Above the ceiling was another room, and above that the roof and, above the roof, the heavens. *Which is where my mother and father are*, she thought – *in heaven, if I am to believe what I'm taught. Even if their bodies lie at the bottom of the Atlantic Ocean. Or what is left of their bodies.*

She turned her head to look at the photograph of them both that stood upon her bedside table. Then she burst into floods of tears.

9

Looking back years later, Binnie realized what a landmark that Sunday had been, not just because of the success of the service of remembrance, which had been all she had hoped it would be, but because it was on that evening that she had broken down and wept so bitterly.

She saw that storm of tears as a turning point. Then, suddenly, she grew up.

Ever since the terrible news of the *Titanic*, she

had been trying to play the role of captain of her own family ship, to navigate through troubled waters and find safe harbour. But the strain, that Sunday evening, had been too much for her.

Yet, strangely, once those tears were dried, she found new strength to haul herself up from the depths of despair, to apply herself more firmly to the task in hand.

One little incident helped greatly. As she lay on her bed that evening, she heard Dodie's voice, calling from down below her third-floor window, 'Bin! Are you up there?'

'What is it?' Binnie called back.

'I've got something to show you,' Dodie said. 'In my shed. Can you come down?'

'I'll be there in five minutes,' Binnie said.

Hastily she got off the bed and went into the bathroom to mop her eyes and sponge her tear-stained face and comb her hair. Hopefully, Dodie would not see that she had been crying.

She need not have worried, for Dodie did not spare her a glance, so preoccupied was she with what she had to show her sister.

She flung open the door of the Labour Ward,

and there was Marjorie with four newborn babies, rough-haired, open-eyed, and seemingly all heads and feet.

'They must have been born while we were all in church,' Dodie said. 'I thought she might have them today. She failed the drainpipe test a week ago.'

'Clever Marjorie!' said Binnie. 'Best day to choose to have babies.'

'Why?' asked Dodie.

'The rhyme,' Binnie replied. 'Don't you remember?

> "The child that is born on the Sabbath day
> Is bonny and blithe and good and gay."'

Best thing for me that could have happened, thought Binnie as she watched Marjorie and her children. *One minute I'm weeping about death and the next I'm smiling about birth. Life goes on whether you're a human being or a guinea pig. So count your blessings.*

And one of my blessings is that we are fortunate enough to live in this dear old house and to have servants to cook and to clean, and to see to the gardens. Less than a year ago, I had no idea of the responsibilities that Mother carried. She may not have had to prepare meals or dust or sweep or polish or dig the garden, but she still had to see that all these things were done and done properly, as I now have to do. How lucky I am that there are such nice people working for me – for us – and that they seem to accept me as mistress of this, our home. I do count my blessings, I really do.

As that summer of 1912 went on, it seemed that the Bone children were indeed blessed.

First, the weather was beautiful.

Second, with Watty's help, Fifi learned to read and so made her entry into the wonderful world of books.

Next, Edward, thanks to the help and enthusiasm of one of the masters at his prep school, became a keen butterfly collector. Net in hand, he hunted the Cotswold hills, gradually building a splendid collection of many beautiful butterflies, and, partly because of this, school became for him a happier place.

Dodie, of course, was happy in her shed with her pets, as was Charles with a cricket bat in his hands and Alec with a good book in his.

As for Binnie, now eighteen, the running of Combe Brindle House became gradually easier. Experience helped, as did all the adults around her. Watty, the old cook who had been with them forever, it seemed, the maids, Whittle the gardener, all treated her now with affection but also with a degree of respect, as the mistress of the house.

The people of Combe Brindle too were admiring, it seemed, of her efforts. There was usually a goodish crowd of churchgoers at St Margaret's on a Sunday morning, and afterwards many of them had a cheery word for the Bone children or at the least a nod and a smile.

The Vicar, waiting at his church door as his congregation left, always spoke with Watty and with each of the six children, and every week Binnie looked forward to his handshake and his smile. Robin Seymour had a dry and somewhat quirky sense of humour, and Binnie often laughed at what he had to say.

One Sunday in August, as she walked down to church with her two sisters and her three brothers, she said to herself that although their mother and father had only been dead for a matter of four months, yet already there were more happiness in the Bone family. *None of us has forgotten them for a moment*, she thought, *but we are learning to live with our loss.*

Uncannily, that morning the Vicar's sermon was on this very theme: that though sadness, tragedy even, are a part of all our lives, yet through our own efforts – and with God's help – we can overcome any loss.

Watching Fifi skipping happily ahead as they made their way home after the service, in the bright sunshine of that beautiful August day, and half-listening to the chatter of the rest, Binnie told herself that, from now on, things were going to become steadily better.

When they reached the house, one of the maids came to her to say that there had been a telephone message from Mrs Bone.

'From Mrs Bone?' Binnie said. 'Oh, you mean my grandmother.'

'Yes, Miss Binnie. She said, would you telephone her back please as soon as possible.'

The instrument stood in a kind of glass-sided booth in the hall. Binnie asked the operator for the number of Mafeking Towers and waited for the familiar 'Who calls?'

When it came, she said 'Hello, Granny. It's Binnie. We've just got back from church.'

'Binnie,' said Patience Bone in her quiet voice. 'It is about your grandfather, my dear.'

'Grandfather? Is he ill, Granny?' Binnie asked, thinking the General is never ill, he's as fit as a man half his age.

'No,' said Granny Bone. 'He is not ill. There has been an accident. He was thrown from his horse on the road. It shied at something. I do not want you to tell the other children yet, but your grandfather is dead.'

10

The funeral of General Hereward Bone was quite a grand occasion.

It took place in a great abbey. A bishop gave the sermon, and a number of senior army officers attended. The General's coffin, draped in the Union flag, was carried by four smartly turned out pall-bearers, troopers of his old regiment. At the graveside, a bugler sounded the Last Post.

The Vicar of Combe Brindle came to the funeral, and afterwards, at Mafeking Towers, he said to the three elder Bone children, 'Your grandmother was magnificent, wasn't she? She is a brave old lady.'

'She looked so small, walking behind the coffin,' Binnie said.

'How will she manage on her own?' Robin Seymour asked.

'Our two aunts are going to stay with her for the time being,' Alec said.

'And she can always come and visit us,' Charles said.

'She will like that, I'm sure,' said the Vicar. 'By the way, Charles, how did the cricket go last term?'

'Oh, all right,' replied Charles.

'He's being modest, Mr Seymour,' Alec said. 'He played for the Colts Eleven and he made a lot of runs. Guess what his top score was?'

'Fifty, Charles?' said the Vicar.

Charles grinned.

'No, sir,' he said. 'I got a century.'

'A hundred and five not out!' said Binnie.

'Father would have been proud of him, don't you think?'

'I certainly do,' said the Vicar, 'and if you'll allow me to say so, I'm proud of you all for the way you're coping with another loss so soon after the first. Now then, I must go and find Mrs Bone.'

Smiling, he shook hands with the three of them, and Binnie thought, not for the first time, what a nice smile he had.

'God bless you all,' he said.

As Robin Seymour moved off to find one grandmother, they saw the other one making for them, and Alec and Charles, without a word spoken, slipped away, leaving Binnie to contend with Granny Fea alone. Both boys were too nice-natured to be deliberately disrespectful towards their grandmother, but each felt that on this particular day, such a hard one for Granny Bone, he wanted to avoid having to listen to Granny Fea's empty-headed chatter.

'Oh Binnie,' she said now, 'what a splendid service, wasn't it, with those soldiers in their nice uniforms and the flag on the coffin and all those nice things the Bishop said? He would have been so pleased, the General would.'

Alec and Charles, hungry as growing boys are, made for the food, which was set out on some large trestle tables, and helped themselves to sausage rolls.

'Poor old Bin,' Alec said. 'We really shouldn't have deserted her like that. Look at Granny Fea now, chattering away like a magpie.'

'D'you think she's sweet on the Vicar?' said Charles with his mouth full.

'Who, Granny Fea?'

'No, you chump – Binnie. I was watching her when he shook her hand just now and I thought she went a bit pink.'

'You're imagining it,' Alec said. 'Anyway, he's miles too old for her.'

'How old is he?'

'Don't know.'

'Hello, boys,' said a voice behind them, and they turned to see Grandpa Reggie.

'Grandpa,' said Alec, 'are you good at guessing people's ages?'

'Brilliant,' said Reggie Fea. 'I should say

71

that you, Alec, are nearly seventeen, and you, Charles, are fifteen.'

'Yes, but you knew that,' said Alec. 'How about – let's see . . . um – how about the Vicar for instance? How old would you say he was?'

'Oh, I should think he's pretty ancient,' said Grandpa Reggie.

Alec looked at his brother and nodded, as if to say, 'Told you so.'

'What, d'you mean like . . . thirty?' Charles asked.

Grandpa Reggie smiled.

'Something like that,' he said. 'Why?'

'Oh, just wondered,' Charles said.

At that point, Fifi came running towards them, followed by Edward and Nanny Watts, and Grandpa Reggie scooped up his youngest grand-child and gave her a hug. Fifi had been christened Fiona, but Reggie Fea had his own name for her.

'Fionabone!' he said. 'You're looking very smart.'

'It's my new frock. For the funeral. It cost lots of money, didn't it, Watty?' Fifi said as Nanny Watts joined them.

'Worth every penny,' said Grandpa Reggie. 'You look very nice in it, Fionabone.'

'My other grandfather has gone to Heaven,' Fifi said in a conversational tone. 'When are you going to Heaven, Grandpa Reggie?'

'I'm not in a hurry,' said Reggie Fea, and as the child ran off he asked Nanny Watts, 'Has she yet realized what happened to her mother and father?'

'Yes, I think so,' Watty replied. 'At least there's no more talk about them being on an iceberg. Heaven, I told her, is nice and warm, and she's much happier with that.'

'She likes the idea of them flying,' Alec said.

'Flying?'

'Yes,' said Charles. 'Angels have wings, so everyone in Heaven has wings too, Fifi thinks.'

How I'd love to fly! he thought. *In an aeroplane – I mean a Sopwith Camel, perhaps. Lovely little biplanes they are! I can just see myself whizzing about in one of those.*

Reggie Fea meanwhile was holding a large spotted handkerchief in front of his face, supposedly to blow his nose but actually to conceal

73

the expression upon his face at the thought of the General beating about Heaven with a huge pair of wings, his long legs stuck out behind him like a flamingo.

Very wrong of me, he said to himself. *Very disrespectful to the poor fellow.*

'That's ridiculous,' said Edward.

'What is?' asked Grandpa Reggie. (*Hope he's not a mind-reader*, he thought.)

'The idea of people flying,' Edward said. 'They would need the most enormous wings to keep themselves airborne. People are heavy. They're not like butterflies, you know.'

'How's the collection going, Edward?' Reggie Fea asked.

'Pretty well,' Edward replied. 'Which reminds me, Grandpa, I brought something to show you,' and he put a hand in his pocket and took out a small flattish box and opened it.

Inside, neatly mounted on a stiff cream card, was the spread shape of quite a large butterfly.

Its velvety wings were brownish-black with a lovely sheen of purple and marked with white spots and stripes; on each hind-wing was a black spot with a tawny ring around it, like an eye.

'That,' said Grandpa Reggie, 'is quite beautiful. What is it, Edward?'

'It's a Purple Emperor. I caught it on Rodborough Common.'

And you killed it, thought his grandfather. *Thoughtful, sensitive boy that you are, yet you caught it in your butterfly-net and then put it inside a poison-jar and killed it. But now you have it to keep and to look at.*

We shall not see the General again, nor George, nor my dear daughter Henrietta, but you will have your beautiful Purple Emperor to cherish for the rest of your life.

11

Almost exactly a year later, in August 1913, Binnie Bone sat in her office in Combe Brindle House, thinking back to the General's funeral. She was in the room which had been George Bone's study. As the eldest of the six children and in her adopted role of mistress of the house, she had taken it over. The others referred to it as 'Binnie's office' and it stuck.

She sat now in a swivel-chair at the big roll-top desk, wondering how twelve months could possibly have gone by so quickly. Such a lot seemed to have happened too.

The first thing to be done had been to engage a new governess for Dodie and Fifi, as the retired schoolteacher had now decided to retire completely. Binnie had interviewed a number of applicants, and had chosen a Miss Hopkins, firstly because she wore her hair in a bun like Watty and looked a bit like her too, and secondly because she had a very nice smile, like the Vicar.

The next big test was organizing the celebrations of Christmas 1912. Granny Bone had come to stay and the Fea grandparents had driven over for Christmas dinner. Binnie, looking at all the faces round the dining-room table, from Grandpa Reggie at the opposite end to her to the Afterthought beside her with the doll Florence on her lap, thought that everyone looked happy despite all they had been through.

Then, early in the New Year of 1913, came probate, when her father's will was proven and she now had, from his estate, the monies for school fees and household bills and clothes and so forth, which, up till then, Grandpa Reggie had been paying. Binnie had wanted to pay him back for all the expense to which he had been put, but he flatly refused to accept a penny.

Next, in May, there had been Watty's fiftieth birthday party. All the children had been determined that she should have a really special party, and all had bought her carefully chosen presents. The cook had made a magnificent birthday cake (with five candles, one for each decade), slices of which would be sent by post to the three boys away at school. Everyone else at Combe Brindle House came to the party – Binnie, Dodie, Fifi, Grandpa Reggie and the two grandmothers. Miss Hopkins (already known as 'Hoppy'), the cook, the maids, Whittle the gardener and Mrs Whittle – and the Vicar, too, was asked.

'Shall I invite the Vicar?' Binnie had said to Watty, who replied, 'Certainly'.

There had been other birthdays, of course, during those twelve months. With six of them, seven with Watty and now eight with Hoppy, there seemed to be birthdays all the time, and at

Watty's party they had learned of yet another one, thanks to Fifi, curious as usual.

'When's your birthday?' she had asked the Vicar and he had said, 'September the first, Fifi, and yours is September the tenth.'

'How d'you know that?' she asked.

'I know all your birthdays,' said the Vicar, 'because they're all written down in a book I've got.'

'Because, Fionabone,' said Grandpa Reggie, 'you were all christened at St Margaret's Church.'

'Did you christen me?' Fifi asked the Vicar.

'No, I've only been here three years.'

'Oh,' said Fifi. 'How old are you?'

'You can't ask questions like that,' Watty said.

'Why not?'

'It's rude,' said Hoppy.

'No, no,' said the Vicar. 'I don't mind a bit. I shall be thirty next birthday.'

Now Binnie, sitting in her office and recalling this, was thinking, *We must remember to send a card to Mr Seymour on September the first. Funny, I don't know why I call him that. I'm nineteen now so he's only eleven years older and he's always called me Binnie, so why don't I call him Robin?*

She was still asking herself this at the end of August. If a birthday card was to be bought, it must be done now.

What sort of birthday card, she wondered, do you send to a clergyman? Does it have to be religious? Or could it be just a country scene, suitable for the vicar of a Somerset village?

In the village stores, which sold everything from cheese to chocolate, from bread and biscuits to stamps and stationery, she found a card that seemed to meet all requirements. It showed a photograph of Wells Cathedral – beauty, Somerset and Christianity, all in one.

It was not strictly a birthday card, so Binnie spent some time in her office, considering what she would write in it.

Happy Birthday! Many happy returns of the day? Or maybe just a message from them all, sending their good wishes, their congratulations, their love?

But what to call him? Dear Vicar? Dear Mr Seymour? Dear Robin? *No, I can't put that,* Binnie said to herself. *The others will tease me unmercifully.*

But then, she suddenly thought, *the others don't need to know – they've all forgotten about his birthday anyway, I expect.*

So on the card with the picture of Wells Cathedral, she wrote:

Dear Robin,
We all wish you a very enjoyable thirtieth birthday and many happy returns of it.
    With love from Fifi, Dodie, Edward, Charles, Alec and Binnie Bone.

12

On Robin Seymour's thirtieth birthday he received, much to his surprise, a great many cards. Some were from his family – his mother and father, his brothers and sisters, aunts, uncles, cousins – and some from friends. He particularly liked the one from the Bone children at Combe Brindle House. *Though one can't call Binnie a child any more*, he said to himself. But he had not expected so many birthday cards from his parishioners. Someone (*I wonder who*, he thought) seemed to have broadcast the date around the village, and on September the first there were cards from almost every member of his congregation.

In the Vicarage dining-room where the Seymour family was sitting down to a birthday lunch, there were cards on the mantelpiece, on occasional tables, on window-sills, on bookshelves.

'Anyone would think,' said the Vicar's father, 'that it was your hundredth birthday. I'm surprised you haven't had a telegram from His Majesty the King.'

'I think it's lovely,' his mother said. 'People must think very well of you, Robin.'

'I expect,' said one of his older brothers, 'that most of them are from young ladies. He's probably the pick of the eligible bachelors of Combe Brindle. Many a young woman would dearly like to become the Vicar's wife, I dare say.'

'Oh rubbish!' said Robin Seymour, smiling, but all the same he could not resist a quick glance at one particular card on the mantelpiece – a card showing the west front of Wells Cathedral.

Nine days later it was Fifi's birthday, her seventh, and there was another party, at Combe Brindle House. Her brothers had gone back to school – all now at Marlborough, Alec in his last term, Edward in his first – so the guests were her two sisters and Watty and Hoppy, and in addition she had been allowed to invite four friends.

She had chosen three small girls and Binnie had said, 'One more. Who else would you like to have?'

'The Vicar,' replied the Afterthought.

'The Vicar? Why?'

'I like him.'

'Seems a good reason,' Watty said.

'You like him, don't you, Bin?' Fifi asked.

'Of course,' said Binnie. 'We all do.'

'And he'll be useful,' Dodie said.

'Useful? How?'

'Well, he can play the piano, can't he?'

'Yes.'

'Well then, we can have musical chairs.'

*

Soon Christmas 1913 was upon them, and this time they all went to Littledown Manor (by Rolls-Royce) to spend it with Grandpa Reggie and Granny Fea.

Perhaps because it was Christmas, and they'd all grown a little older and a little more tolerant, they found Granny Fea a little less maddening than usual. In fact they decided she could be quite funny (on purpose or by mistake) and they laughed at her jokes and at Grandpa Reggie's imitations.

Out of respect for Granny Bone he did not, of course, do his take-off of the General, but he did impressions of a number of people who they all knew. He was not only good at voices but also at copying gestures and the way people walked. Everyone laughed themselves silly when he did a perfect imitation of his wife, at the end of which she said, 'Who was that meant to be, Reggie?'

'You haven't done the Vicar, Grandpa,' Charles said. He watched Binnie as he spoke, hoping that perhaps she would blush, but she smiled at him quite naturally.

'Our Vicar here?' said Grandpa Reggie.

'No,' said Charles. '*Our* Vicar.'

'Oh, Harold, you mean?'

'*Harold?*'

For answer Reggie Fea drew himself up to his full height (such as it was) and placing his hands together he declaimed, in a fair copy of Robin Seymour's voice,

'Our Vicar
Which art not yet in Heaven
Harold be Thy Name.'

'Reggie!' squawked Granny Fea. 'You cannot say that! Whatever would Mr Seymour say if he knew?'

'Probably,' said Granny Bone in her soft voice, 'he'd have a good laugh.'

'And he'd think I was crackers,' said Grandpa Reggie. 'Talking of which, let's pull 'em.'

As they sat round the table, now wearing paper hats and reading out the mottoes that had come from the crackers, there was laughter as they drank their wine or ginger pop or lemonade, according to age.

Once again, looking round at the family as she had done at Christmas a year ago, Binnie thought that though they hadn't forgotten the faces that now were missing, at any rate they all seemed to be making a show of being happy. She caught Granny Bone's eye and they smiled at one another, each confident that she was thinking exactly the same thing.

The year 1914 began just like any other year. No one in the family, at Combe Brindle House, at Littledown Manor, at Mafeking Towers, had the faintest idea that towards the end of the coming summer, on 4 August, their world would suddenly be turned upside down.

They could have had no suspicion that, for the next four years, the blast of war would blow in their ears, and millions of young lives would be wasted.

13

On April Fool's Day 1914, almost two years since the death of their parents, Dodie and Fifi were in the shed, cleaning out the hutches of the rabbits and guinea pigs. A younger sister of Marjorie, Monica by name, had just produced three big-headed babies, and the subject of reproduction came up.

'Dodie,' Fifi said, 'I know how babies are born.'

'Do you?' said Dodie. 'Tell me, then.'

'Well,' said Fifi, 'you have to have a mummy and a daddy. Mummies can't do it by themselves. And then you have to have a stork.'

'A stork?'

'Yes, Hoppy told me,' said Fifi. 'I asked her how people get babies and she said, "A stork brings the baby," and I said, "What, in its beak?" and she said, "No, the baby is wrapped in a cloth and the stork holds the end of the cloth in its beak," and I said, "Where do storks come from?" and she said, "Holland mostly". So you see, most babies come from Holland.'

Dodie pointed at Monica's newborn children.

'These didn't,' she said.

'I expect it's different for guinea pigs,' Fifi said. 'I'll ask Hoppy.'

She put fresh sawdust into one of the hutches and then she said, 'Hoppy has never had a baby.'

'No,' said Dodie.

'Nor Watty.'

'Well, neither of them is married.'

'I shall get married when I'm grown up,' Fifi

said, 'and have lots of babies. Like Monica and Marjorie. Will you, Dodie?'

'I might do.'

'And Binnie might, too.'

'Yes, she might.'

'Gosh!' said Fifi. 'We're going to need an awful lot of storks.'

In her office, Binnie was not thinking of birth but of death. The second anniversary of that telephone call with its dreadful news was almost upon them, *And however long I live*, she thought, *however many birthdays I have, I shall never forget Mother and Father's deathday.*

At that precise moment she heard the telephone in the hall ringing, remembering also, as she went to answer it, that other dreadful call, from Granny Bone. Now it was indeed Granny Bone on the line.

'Binnie dear,' she said. 'How are you?'

'Fine, Granny.'

'And the other children?'

'We're all well, thank you, and how are you?'

'I'm very well, dear, but I do have a big favour to ask of you. It isn't really something that we can discuss over the telephone, so would you consider coming over here whenever is convenient for you? I can send Phillips over with the dogcart.'

'Yes, of course, Granny,' Binnie said. 'Tomorrow if you like.'

'Say ten o'clock then, and you can stay for lunch and then Phillips will drive you home again.'

So next morning the old General's groom, an ex-trooper of his regiment, helped Binnie into the dogcart and flourished his whip at the pony and away they went at a spanking rate.

It was a lovely spring morning and Binnie enjoyed the ten-mile trip between greening hedges, especially when she not only saw some early swallows but also heard the first cuckoo of the year. *What's this favour that Granny's going to ask?* she said to herself. Soon she found out, sitting in the great, high, ugly drawing-room at Mafeking Towers.

'I wonder,' Granny Bone said, 'if you would consider having me to stay at Combe Brindle House for a while?'

'Of course, Granny!'

'You see,' said Granny Bone, 'I've at last made my mind up to sell Mafeking Towers.'

'Sell it?'

'Yes. Since Hereward died, I've been rattling around like a pea in a drum, in this great barracks of a place. To be honest with you, Binnie, I have never liked it. What I'm planning to do is to find a nice little cottage, preferably a bit nearer to all of you. But that might take a bit of time. So, once I've sold this house, could I come to you? Hopefully it wouldn't be for too long.'

'As long as you like, Granny,' Binnie said.

'Thank you, dear, thank you so much.'

Father would be glad, thought Binnie as she bowled home in the dogcart, to think of her coming here. *Though I'm not sure the General would be too happy about the sale of that 'great barracks'.*

In fact that sale took place early in June, to a wealthy Bristol businessman who saw Mafeking Towers as the sort of country seat from which he might mix with the upper classes, the county folk, maybe even the nobility, and on 28 June 1914, Patience Bone arrived to stay at Combe Brindle House with her grandchildren. Also on 28 June (as the next day's newspapers reported), a certain Archduke Franz Ferdinand, heir to the Austro-Hungarian throne, was assassinated.

14

There was turmoil in Europe, and it was Germany's attack upon Belgium that brought Great Britain into the conflict.

On 4 August 1914, war was declared upon the Germans, and the first British soldiers were sent to France. The call went out for the young men of the British Isles to fight for King and Country, and many hurried to enlist.

In the Bone family, the three grandsons of the late General Hereward Bone reacted differently.

Alec had just enough of the General's blood in his veins to say to himself that there was really no question about it; he had better join the Army. He was not by nature a particularly bold person but the romantic in him dreamed of doing something splendid, like taking part in a cavalry charge, the reins in one hand as he whirled his sabre around his head amid the thunder of hoofs.

His ideas of warfare were squarely based on the tales told to them all, when small, by the General, about the Boers in South Africa, who would not come out into the open and fight man to man, but hid behind cover and sniped at the brave British soldiers.

'But weren't the Boers brave too, Grandfather?' the boys asked.

'Certainly not!' the General replied. 'Cowards to a man. Slinking about in their dirty colourless clothes so that you had a job to pick them out, not like our gallant fellows in their bright uniforms.'

Alec, now eighteen, was in his last year at

Marlborough. He had planned to go on to university, but once war had been declared, most of his friends could not wait to leave school and enlist, in the Army or the Navy, or even in some cases in the newly established Royal Flying Corps.

I can't be the odd man out, Alec told himself. *I must go too*.

As for Charles, the idea of joining up to fight the Germans was instantly appealing, for he was more like the General than either of his brothers.

'I may be only sixteen,' he said to himself, 'but what's to stop me saying I'm older?'

To Edward, at thirteen, the declaration of war meant little. He'd been much too small to be influenced by the General's stories and hadn't listened to them much anyway, and now, obviously, he was too young to worry. Nevertheless, he did worry. To kill, and then to stick a pin through the body of one of his beloved butterflies, caused him no problems. But the notion of killing another human being, perhaps by sticking a bayonet into a man's body, was something he could not bear to think of.

'Ah well,' he thought, 'this war will be over in a few months or at any rate long before I'm old enough to have to do anything.'

Back at home at Combe Brindle House for the summer holidays, each of the Bone boys spent his time differently.

Edward spent his days butterfly net in hand, poison-jar at the ready.

Charles, now an accepted and most welcome member of the Combe Brindle village cricket team, played the game as often as possible, and scored a great many boundaries.

Alec looked for advice. Normally, despite being a boy and only a year younger, he went to Binnie with any run-of-the-mill problem, but this was different. She was a girl, after all, and girls knew nothing about war. He felt deeply the lack of a father to consult. Not that George Bone would have known anything much about soldiering, despite being a General's son, but he would have had advice to offer, suggestions to put forward. It's not always easy to make your mind up about a major decision if you're only eighteen, and Alec needed help, even if it was only in the shape of an opinion. He went to see Grandpa Reggie.

Littledown Manor was a bit further away than Mafeking Towers, more like twenty miles than ten in fact, but Alec rode over on his bicycle on an August morning so bright and warm and filled with the beauty of the West country that it seemed impossible to believe that there was a war on, although at that very time a great battle was being fought, at Mons, as a result of which the British Army stemmed the Germans advancing into France.

Granny Fea and Grandpa Reggie welcomed Alec, the former with open arms and much shrill laughter, the latter with a firm shake of the hand of the grandson now grown taller than himself. They looked very different, the long-legged fair-haired youth and the short dark tubby man, now fast approaching seventy.

'What can we do for you, Alec, dear boy?' Grandpa Reggie enquired.

'I need your advice,' Alec said.

'Come and sit down,' said Reggie Fea. 'You must be exhausted, cycling all that way. I know I should be.'

'So should I be, I'm sure!' giggled Granny Fea.

'You would, Felicity, you would,' said her husband. 'Now, do you think you could arrange for this intrepid traveller to have something to eat and drink, while he and I are having a little chat?'

'Of course, Reggie.'

'Off you go then, my dear,' said Grandpa Reggie, and when she had left the room, 'Now then, Alec, what's this all about?'

'Grandpa,' said Alec, 'I've been thinking. I think I ought to join the Army.'

'Ought to?'

'Well, lots of my friends are going to.'

'You want to leave school and enlist?'

'I don't want to but I think I should.'

'Do you plan a career as a professional soldier, like your other grandfather?'

'Oh no.'

'But you want to cut short your education and go and fight the Germans?'

'Yes. Unless you think I'm being silly, Grandpa?'

Reggie Fea sighed.

'No,' he said, 'I don't think you're being silly. I think you're behaving admirably. Perhaps I had better contact your housemaster at school and acquaint him with your plans? You can't just push off without telling anybody.'

'Oh yes, please, could you?'

'And what body of soldiery do you plan to join, pray? A West Country regiment, I trust? The Gloucesters? The Wiltshires?'

'No,' said Alec. 'My own county, I think. The Somerset Yeomanry are asking for recruits. I saw the notice in the Recruiting Office in Bath.'

'Then go to Bath,' said Reggie Fea, 'and the best of British luck to you. You can have a lift there in my car. I bet you'll be the first volunteer to arrive in a Rolls-Royce Silver Ghost.'

15

'Well, thanks, Grandpa,' Alec said. 'I mean thanks for the advice and thanks for the offer of a lift in the Rolls, but I think I'd better cycle home first. I want to sleep on the idea, and anyway I'd better tell Binnie before I do anything.'

'Have a word with the head of the family, you mean?' Grandpa Reggie said.

'Well, yes, I suppose so.'

'Quite right, Alec, and I'll tell you exactly what she'll say.'

'What?'

'She'll say, "It's your decision."'

'It's your decision,' Binnie said when Alec came into her office and told her of his plans.

He'll have to do his training first, she thought, *and by the time he's ready to be sent abroad, the war may be over.*

'When are you going to do it?' she asked.

'I'll go into Bath tomorrow,' Alec said.

Next morning he was out in the coach-house, pumping up his tyres, when Charles sauntered in, bat in one hand, cricket ball in the other.

'Care to bowl to me?' he asked.

'Sorry,' Alec said. 'Haven't got time. I'm going into Bath.'

'What for?'

'I'm going to join up, Charles,' Alec said. 'I've decided to leave Marlborough and enlist. A lot of my friends are going to do the same.'

'You're going to join the Army?' Charles said.

'Yes.'

'What regiment?'

'The Somerset Yeomanry, if I can. I'm off to the Recruiting Office.'

'Where's that?' asked Charles.

'On the corner of Queen's Square.'

'Oh. Well, good luck,' said Charles and stuck out his hand and Alec shook it. Despite some twenty months difference in age, the two brothers looked very alike, both fair-haired, both the same height, for Charles, though the younger, promised before long to be the taller.

'Thanks,' Alec said. 'Right, see you later. I'm off,' and he cycled away down the drive.

Half an hour later, another cyclist left Combe Brindle House and took the Bath road. As he pedalled along on his machine, his thoughts were of other machines – flying machines.

In the office on the corner of Queen's Square the Recruiting Sergeant took down Alec's details – name, address, religion, next of kin, date of birth.

'Right, sonny,' he said. 'You'm old enough. I reckon, nearly nineteen. I've had a lot of eighteen-year-olds come in, wanting to have a go at they Germans. Now then, what's it to be?'

'I beg your pardon, sir?' said Alec.

'"Sergeant" it is, sonny. I don't get to be "Sir" till I'm a warrant officer, which I bain't. Yet. What I'm saying is, you've got the whole bleedin' British Army to choose from. Which mob d'ye want to join?'

'Oh, the Somerset Yeomanry, please, sergeant.'

'Why's that, then?'

'I'm Somerset born.'

'Good enough reason,' said the Recruiting Sergeant. 'Right then, I've got all I wants. In a few days you'll get your orders, which will be to report to the Yeomanry Headquarters down in Taunton. Now then, off you goes back home to say goodbye to your ma and pa.'

If only I could! thought Alec as he left the Recruiting Office and mounted his bicycle. Preoccupied with his thoughts, he did not notice another cyclist who was standing beside his machine behind one of the trees in the middle of the square.

Hardly had the Recruiting Sergeant half-smoked a Woodbine (NO SMOKING said the notice on the wall behind the desk) than in came another volunteer, another tall fair-haired youth.

The Sergeant stubbed out his cigarette.

'Right, sonny,' he said.

He opened his record book.

'What's your name, then?' he asked.

'Bone,' said Charles. 'Charles Bone.'

'Bone?' said the Sergeant. 'I've just had somebody in by that name. Not ten minutes ago.'

He looked in the book.

'Alec Bone,' he said. 'Enlisted in the Somerset Yeomanry.'

'My brother,' Charles said.

'Combe Brindle House, Combe Brindle?' the Recruiting Sergeant asked.

'Yes.'

'Your older brother?'

'Yes.'

'Thought so. You look a sight younger, you do.'

'Not much,' Charles said.

'Ah, come on now, sonny,' said the Sergeant. 'I'll bet you'm no more than fifteen or sixteen.

'Tis praiseworthy you wanting to join up at your age, but you'm too young.'

'We're twins, Alec and I are,' said Charles.

'But you just said he was your older brother.'

'So he is. Ten minutes older.'

'When's your birthday, then?'

'September the twenty-third, 1896.'

The Recruiting Sergeant looked long and hard at Charles. He sighed, and then, shaking his head, he dipped his pen in the inkwell.

'All right then, sonny,' he said. 'So you're for the Somerset Yeomanry too, eh?'

'No,' said Charles. 'Please, I want to join the Royal Flying Corps.'

16

By the middle of September 1914 things had changed, both on the great stage of the war in Europe and in the little world of the Bone family.

In France, the British Army was fighting another great battle, to stop the Germans' attempt to push on into French territory. In August there had been the Battle of Mons, in September the Battle of the Marne.

Now, in Combe Brindle House, things looked very different. The three boys were gone as usual, but not, except in the case of Edward, back to school.

Alec was on the barracks square at the Somerset Yeomanry's Taunton headquarters.

Charles, still not yet seventeen, was stationed a great deal further away, at Cranwell in Lincolnshire. Like his brother, he was learning to march and to turn and to wheel, to form fours, to mark time, to halt, and lastly, thankfully, to stand at ease. Like his brother, he was at the mercy of non-commissioned officers who shouted endlessly at him and his mates. Dreams they might all have had of being taught to fly an aeroplane were still just dreams. Flying was a long way ahead.

For Binnie, proud as she was of Alec and Charles, the knowledge of the dangers each would have to face some day soon was a constant anxiety. The casualty lists in the newspapers were increasing, and among the dead and the wounded were already some names that she knew, of soldiers from Combe Brindle.

Binnie had faith of the simplest sort – faith in

God's goodness, a belief that if she put her trust in Him, all would be well. But then she thought, *What of other people, believers like herself, whose sons, be they English, French or German, had already laid down their lives for their countries? How could her faith protect her brothers when their turn came to face the foe?*

One Sunday she chanced to be the last person to leave the church after morning service. As she came out of the door, the Vicar was shaking hands with one final couple of worshippers, who then walked off down the churchyard path.

'What news of the boys, Binnie?' he asked.

'Not much, I'm afraid,' Binnie said. 'They're neither of them the world's best correspondent. One letter from each so far, both moaning about the food and the endless drill.'

'At least,' said the Vicar, 'they're safe from shot and shell for the time being. I saw in the lists in yesterday's *Times* another Combe Brindle casualty – Ted Bull, the blacksmith's son.'

'Killed?'

'Missing, believed killed.'

'Robin –' began Binnie and then she blushed – 'Oh, I'm sorry, I shouldn't call you that.'

'Why ever not? I've called you by your Christian name ever since I've known you,' said Robin Seymour. 'What was it you were going to say?'

'You believe in the goodness of God, don't you?'

'I do.'

'Then how can He let these awful things happen? Ted Bull's mother and father must have prayed to God to keep their son safe but it didn't do any good, did it? When Alec and Charles do go to war and I pray, as I shall, that they come to no harm, what good shall I be doing?'

Her eyes filled with tears, and the Vicar took one of her hands in his own and held it, gently.

'Only God knows the answer to that, Binnie,' he said. 'But as I said to you not long ago, I believe very strongly in the power of prayer. Promise me you won't try to do without it, will you?'

Binnie nodded. She wiped her eyes and blew her nose and said, 'I must be going home. I told Dodie I'd pick some dandelions for her animals.'

'Make me one more promise before you go,' the Vicar said.

'What?'

'That from now on you will always call me Robin. Will you do that?'

Binnie smiled.

'Yes, Robin,' she said.

When Binnie arrived home with a big bunch of dandelions, she found not only Dodie but also Fifi busy in the shed. Partly out of her own good nature, partly because she was glad of the help, Dodie had appointed the Afterthought as Rabbit Keeper, leaving her a little freer to concentrate upon her beloved guinea pigs. *It somehow seemed to balance things out better*, Binnie thought, *for Dodie, the least talkative Bone, had the conversational guinea pigs to look after while the wordy Fifi chattered endlessly to the silent rabbits.*

As Binnie entered the house, she heard the ringing of the telephone and then, as she neared it, saw Granny Bone standing in the booth and heard her say in her soft voice, 'Who calls?' and then, 'Would you hold the line a moment? I'll see if I can find her.'

'I'm here, Granny,' Binnie called. 'Who is it?'

'A lady telephoning from Marlborough,' Granny Bone said.

'From the school, you mean?'

'Yes.'

Binnie took the receiver, thinking, *It must be something about Edward. Not bad news, please, God!*

Sunday lunch at Combe Brindle House was, as always, a traditional one – roast beef and Yorkshire pudding, usually followed by Spotted Dick and custard or treacle pudding.

In the absence of Alec, to whom she would have given the job, Binnie set about carving the sirloin of beef. Then, when all had been served – Granny Bone at the far end of the long rectangular dining-table, Nanny Watts and Fifi on one side, Miss Hopkins and Dodie on the other – she took her seat at the head of the table.

'What was the telephone call from Marlborough about, Binnie dear?' asked Granny Bone.

'Oh, it was to say that Edward is in the sanatorium.'

'He is ill?'

'No, not very,' said Binnie, 'but not in a

particularly good temper apparently. He's itching like mad.'

'Itching?' said Granny Bone. 'Why?'

'He's got chicken-pox.'

17

The only one in the family with the immediate means, financial and mechanical, to travel to Marlborough to visit Edward was Grandpa Reggie, and this, to everyone's surprise, he now planned to do.

On hearing the news of his grandson's illness, he had recalled, with painful clarity, the irritation and vexation which chicken-pox had caused him as a child nearly sixty years before.

I shall go and see the boy, he said to himself, *and take him some presents to cheer him up.*

'So, Felicity,' he said to his wife, 'I'm going to drive up and visit young Edward. Take him some gifts, y'know.'

'Oh Reggie, what a nice idea!' cried Granny Fea. 'I'll come with you.'

Grandpa Reggie was, however, ready for this.

'You told me that you had never had chicken-pox,' he said.

'No, I never did.'

'In that case, my dear, it would be most unwise of you to accompany me. Catching it from the boy would be very uncomfortable for you, not to say dangerous at your time of life.'

Without regret then, Reggie Fea set off alone next day – alone, that is, except for Toghill the chauffeur and he was separated from his master by the glass panel that divided driver from passengers in the Silver Ghost.

Toghill's instructions were first to drive into Bath, in which city he sprang out of the Rolls three times to open the rear door and help his passenger out – first at a sweet shop, then at a book shop and, lastly, at a large grocery story.

A passing small boy, gazing open-mouthed at the beautiful motor-car, saw the uniformed chauffeur help his master back into the rear seat and place a number of parcels beside him, tuck a rug carefully round the legs of his short tubby passenger, touch his cap and take the wheel.

Reggie Fea lifted the mouthpiece of the voice-tube that ran through the glass panel.

'To Marlborough, Toghill,' he said. 'Wake me when we arrive,' and he settled himself comfortably for sleep.

Eastward went the Rolls, through the towns of Chippenham and Calne and then up over the Wiltshire downs, finally drawing up outside the school sanatorium.

There were six boys with chicken-pox, and five of them watched with envy the arrival of Bone's grandfather, followed by the tall figure of Toghill, bearing gifts.

'Now then, Edward,' said Grandpa Reggie, 'here's Father Christmas come early. I've brought a few things you might like.'

'Oh Grandpa!' said Edward. 'Can I open them?'

'Of course you can.'

Reggie Fea knew well that growing boys are particularly fond of things to eat, and he watched with pleasure as Edward untied string and ripped off wrappings and discovered, to his delight and before the envious gaze of the other inmates, a large fruitcake, a big tin of biscuits, a huge bunch of grapes, a tall jar of toffees and the most enormous box of chocolates. Finally he undid one last flattish parcel and his mouth fell open and his eyes shone. In it was a beautifully bound and lavishly illustrated book entitled *The Butterflies and Moths of the British Isles*.

'Oh Grandpa!' Edward said. 'I wanted this book like anything but I couldn't afford it. Thank you so much, and thank you for all the other things. I feel better already.'

'Good,' said Grandpa Reggie. 'How about opening that box of chocolates, eh, Edward? I wouldn't mind one and I'm sure Toghill wouldn't say no.'

He looked around the room at the other five boys.

'You chaps wouldn't say no either, I'll bet,' he said, and they all grinned at him.

As they prepared to drive home to Littledown Manor, Reggie Fea, swaddled once more in his rug, was struck by a sudden thought. He took up the voice-pipe.

'Toghill,' he said.

'Yes, sir?'

'Have you ever had chicken-pox?'

'No, sir.'

Oh dear, said his employer to himself. *I should have thought of that. Ah well!*

'Drive on,' he said, and leaning back against the cushions, closed his eyes.

18

In the spring of 1915 Granny Bone found just the cottage she had been looking for. It was as different from ugly great old Mafeking Towers as it could possibly be.

It was small and cosy, with a thatched roof and climbing roses growing around the door, just like the cottages you see pictured on postcards or on calendars. There was a small pretty garden and a neat lawn with a mulberry tree standing at its edge, the whole bordered by a white picket fence. There was even, at the lower end, a brook running by, fringed with willows. Better still, Rose Cottage (what else?) stood on the edge of the village of Combe Brindle, no more than a quarter of a mile from the Bones' house.

'It's ideal, Granny, isn't it?' Binnie said.

'It's everything I'd hoped for,' replied Patience Bone. 'Not that your grandfather would have cared for it much,' she mused. 'He'd have been hitting his head every time he came through the door, it's so low. Of course people were much smaller when it was built, a couple of hundred years ago.'

'Good job you're not very tall,' Binnie said. *I just hope you won't be lonely*, she thought, *living there all by yourself.*

Then an idea occurred to her. *Watty*, she said to herself, *Watty's really at a loose end now. Fifi's too old to need a nanny and anyway she's got Hoppy to look after her. How about Watty going to live at Rose Cottage with Granny Bone, as a companion? They always seem to get on well together.*

'When will you be able to move in?' she asked her grandmother.

'In good time for Christmas, I hope.'

'How will you manage with the cooking and the housework? Will you get someone from the village to come in?'

'I dare say.'

'How many bedrooms are there?' Binnie asked.

'Three.'

Enough, Binnie thought. *They can each have their own room and there'll still be a spare room. They'd be company for each other, especially in the long winter evenings, and Watty's always liked pottering about, doing a bit of gardening – she'd be a help there. Shall I suggest it? Or had I better sound out Watty first? No, I'll come straight out with it and see what the reaction is.*

'There's just one thing I'm worried about, Granny,' she said.

'What's that, Binnie dear?'

'I'm worried that you will be lonely.'

'But you'll all be very close.'

'Yes, but wouldn't it be nicer if you had someone living in Rose Cottage with you for company

– someone to talk to, someone to lend a hand generally?'

Granny Bone put her head on one side, looking up at her tall granddaughter.

'Are you hatching a plot, Binnie?' she asked.

'Sort of.'

'And who, pray, is this person who is going to live with me? Have you someone in mind?'

'Yes,' said Binnie, 'I have. Nanny Watts. You like her, don't you?'

'She is a very nice woman,' Granny Bone said. 'We get on very well together. But I shouldn't think she would want to up sticks after all the years she's lived in this house. I don't think it fair to ask her, do you?'

'She can always say no,' Binnie replied.

'She will,' said Granny Bone.

But she was wrong.

Binnie went to Watty's room and found her at work on a piece of embroidery. By a happy chance it was of a typical country scene, of a cottage and its garden, no less.

'That's pretty,' Binnie said. 'You often do that sort of picture, don't you, Watty?'

'When I was younger,' Watty said, 'I used to dream that one day I would live in a cottage like that.'

'With a thatched roof perhaps?' Binnie asked.

'Oh yes.'

'And roses round the door?'

'Yes indeed, and a pretty garden with a stream running by the bottom of it. Just like Rose Cottage in fact. Your grandmother has been telling me all about it. It sounds wonderful.'

'Just the sort of place you'd like to live in?' said Binnie.

'I'd love to.'

'You could.'

'What d'you mean?'

'Granny Bone is going to be lonely, living all by herself with no one to talk to. She's never lived on her own. She might like to have someone sharing Rose Cottage with her. She might ask you if you'd like to.'

'She won't,' said Nanny Watts.

But of course she, too, was wrong.

In the event, it all turned out just as Binnie hoped. Patience and Helen, as Granny Bone and Watty now agreed to call one another, were delighted to discover that they were both happy at the thought of living together in Rose Cottage.

'I think it an excellent plan,' said Patience Bone. 'I have no doubt but that we shall get on like a house on fire.'

Helen Watts smiled.

'Not the happiest of expressions, Patience!' she said. 'But I can't tell you how delighted I am at the thought.'

'That makes two of us. By the way, was all this your idea?'

'No. Binnie's. She said you might like it.'

'She told me that about you.'

They looked at one another and laughed.

19

On a Saturday morning in November, Binnie was sitting at the desk in her office, reading that morning's post, which included letters from Alec in France and from Charles in Lincolnshire. She had heard from neither for a while, consoling herself with the thought that 'no news is good news'. But the news she was to hear a few minutes later was not good.

Looking out of the office window, she saw the figure of the Vicar approaching over the croquet lawn, bare now of the white-painted hoops and bright-coloured posts of the summer game. Binnie went through into the adjoining sitting-room and opened the French windows.

'Good morning, Robin,' she said. 'Do come in. It's a bit nippy out today.'

'Morning, Binnie,' said Robin Seymour. 'Sorry to take you away from your desk.'

'How did you know I was at it?'

'Saw you through your office window as I crossed the lawn. I thought I'd come and tell you a bit of news before everyone gets to know it, tomorrow morning in church.'

'What news?' Binnie asked.

'I'm leaving. Tomorrow's services will be the last I shall take in St Margaret's. For the time being.'

Binnie felt so shocked that she wondered for an instant if she was going to faint. She sat down abruptly on a sofa.

'You're going?' she said, looking dazedly up at the Vicar of Combe Brindle and seeing him smiling down at her as though there was nothing to worry about.

'Yes,' he said.

'To another parish?'

'No. I'm going to join up, I suppose you could say. I'm going to enlist as a chaplain in the Army.'

'But you'll be sent to France.'

'Yes.'

Binnie swallowed.

'But surely you needn't, Robin,' she said. 'You're a clergyman. Your duty is here, isn't it?'

'I shall come back here, God willing,' Robin Seymour said, 'when this war is over, but now I must go and do a different sort of duty,' and he sat down on the sofa beside Binnie and told her how, for months now, he had agonized over the fact that tens of thousands of young men were fighting for their country, risking their lives, while he, because of his calling, was safe and comfortable.

'Had I been older,' he said, 'it would have been a different matter, but I've felt increasingly uncomfortable, knowing that a number of the clergy of my age are already serving as chaplains to the forces. So I went to the Bishop and told

127

him of my decision, and he has appointed an older man to be the vicar here while I'm away.'

Binnie said nothing to this, but sat, her hands pressed together between her knees, her dark head bent.

Looking at her, Robin thought, *For four years now I have known this girl – this woman I must call her now – and from the first liked her, and then became fond of her, and now . . . I love her, I love her dearly. I would she were my wife. I could ask her now, this very minute, but I must not. The Lord alone knows how long I shall be away, or indeed whether I shall come through unscathed. I don't believe it would be right to ask her to wait for me.*

'I didn't want you to hear all this from other people, Binnie,' he said. 'If you were not in church tomorrow, that is.'

'I shall be,' Binnie said.

She stood up and he rose too and she said, 'When will you be leaving?'

'In a week's time,' Robin said. 'By a happy chance I am to be attached to the Somerset Yeomanry, so Alec will be part of my new flock. But I'll come and say goodbye to you all before I go, of course.'

'Don't forget to call in at Rose Cottage too,' Binnie said. 'Granny Bone and Watty are moving in next week.'

'Of course I'll say goodbye to them as well,' said Robin, 'and I'll try to visit Mr and Mrs Fea if I can.'

'But you,' he thought, 'you are the one to whom saying goodbye is going to be so very hard.'

Binnie opened the French windows for him.

'I'll see you in church tomorrow morning,' she said.

And perhaps once or twice next week, she thought, *and then not for ages. Suppose that the worst were to happen and you never came back? Oh Robin, dearest man, if you only knew how much you meant to me! Don't even hold your hand out to me now – just go, before I weep like a child.* And as though he had read her mind, he went out and across the croquet lawn, and turned and waved once, and then disappeared from view.

A little later, Binnie telephoned Littledown Manor. 'Much easier,' she thought, 'if Grandpa Reggie and Granny Fea were to come to

St Margaret's tomorrow. It would save Robin having to travel to them.'

So at Matins the following morning, she sat in the family pew with her two sisters, Miss Hopkins, Granny Bone and Nanny Watts, and the Fea grandparents as well, and looked up at the Vicar of Combe Brindle standing in his pulpit in his white robes.

First he preached his sermon, on friendship and the importance of keeping up old ties, and then he made the announcement of his imminent departure, at which something between a groan and a sigh ran through the congregation, surprised and shocked at this news.

After the service Robin Seymour stood by the door of his church as usual. At his side was the elderly white-haired clergyman who was to take his place for as long as might be necessary.

All wanted to say farewell to their vicar and to express hopes that his absence would not be a long one. A gruff-spoken colonel, an old soldier like the General, gave Robin a piece of advice.

'Look after your feet, Vicar,' he growled. 'A man can't march if his feet are not in first-class condition. Mind and change your socks regularly.'

Then Binnie's turn came to shake hands. As there were people all around, she made herself say, 'This is a great surprise, Vicar,' as though it was the first she had heard of his departure. 'We shall all miss you.'

'I shall miss you all, Miss Bone,' replied Robin Seymour, straight-faced, and then he dropped one eyelid for an instant in what must, Binnie thought, have been a wink.

20

Throughout 1915, the terrible reality of the war began to become clear to the British people at home, as they read in their newspapers of the great battles that were taking place in Europe – battles that showed no advances made, no ground gained, nothing but a huge loss of lives.

In this war trenches were of enormous importance as the main form of protection for the

opposing armies, which faced each other, sometimes no more than fifty metres apart. In relative
safety from small arms fire or shelling, British and
German men lived below ground level.

At Neuve Chapelle, at Ypres, at Loos, the
pattern of trench warfare was established. First
of all, British artillery would fire their guns in a
long and heavy attack upon the German front
lines. Then this would stop and the infantry,
the 'Tommies', would go 'over the top', climbing
out of the comparative safety of their trenches
and walking towards the enemy across No Man's
Land. Whereupon the Germans would direct
a deadly hail of rifle and machine-gun fire upon
the British as they advanced over open ground,
killing or wounding thousands in a very short
space of time.

Day by day the casualty lists grew longer, and
there were few families that did not open their
newspapers in dread, unless of course they had
already received one of those terrible telegrams to
tell them that a son had been 'Killed in Action' or
'Missing, Believed Killed'. Whoever opened the
envelope prayed that it would say 'Wounded',

and many a soldier in the line prayed too, for a 'Blighty' – a wound that would not prove fatal but yet would be serious enough to send him home, to hospital and away from the horror of the trenches.

At Combe Brindle House, at Littledown Manor and at Rose Cottage, the casualty lists were read with growing horror. They anxiously scanned the columns of surnames beginning with B, and indeed with S, for in early December the newly appointed padre of Somerset Yeomanry was ordered to France.

For all the family Christmas 1915 was a muted occasion.

At Combe Brindle House perhaps the only one to enjoy the festivities whole-heartedly was Fifi, still too young to be forever dominated by doubts and fears, but Dodie, Charles (on leave from his base in Lincolnshire), and Edward (on holiday from school) did their best to liven things up. Miss Hopkins had gone to spend Christmas with her aged parents, so that her place at the dining-room table would have been vacant, as would Alec's, but Binnie had managed to persuade Granny Bone and Watty to fill them, and everyone tried hard to enjoy the midday meal just as though it were still peacetime. But Binnie's were not the only ears that heard the noise of the pulling of crackers as the sound of rifle fire.

At church that morning, watching the elderly parson as he preached, Binnie had heard little or nothing of his sermon, so deeply was she thinking of the man who should by rights have been standing in that pulpit. What dangers were he and Alec already in? If only she could have word of them!

Then, at the turn of the year, she did. The postman brought not one but two letters addressed to 'Miss Bone'.

One, from Alec, began 'Dear old Bin' and was determinedly cheerful in tone. The weather was not too bad, the food might have been worse, his fellow troopers were a grand lot of chaps, the battalion was in reserve, in fairly comfortable quarters some miles behind the front line.

Robin Seymour's letter, beginning 'My dear Binnie', said nothing about himself but was full of enquiries about the Bone family in general. Was everyone in good health? How were the new occupants of Rose Cottage settling in? How were Dodie's guinea pigs and was the Afterthought doing well as Rabbit Keeper? He said that he had seen Alec on several occasions and had found out something which Alec himself did not yet know, namely that Trooper Bone was shortly to be promoted to Lance-Corporal Bone. 'He looks fine', he wrote, 'and gives me the most tremendous salute whenever we meet. I have to admit to quite liking being addressed by him as "Sir".'

He hoped that everyone had had a good Christmas, and he gave the address of a Field Sorting Office where he might be reached by letter. He ended:

'May 1916 be as happy a New Year as possible for you, Binnie,

With love from Robin.'

Everyone writes 'With love from', don't they? Binnie thought. *It doesn't mean anything. Still, it's better than 'Yours sincerely'.*

Replying to Alec's letter was easy, Binnie found. She could give him news of Aircraftsman Bone, telling him that Charles had been accepted as a rigger. This meant that he was now responsible for the rigging of some of the biplanes in use by the Royal Flying Corps, such as Sopwith Pups and Camels. He was hopeful that this might eventually lead to his being accepted for training as a pilot. Edward, she wrote, was still equally keen on flying things, his precious butterflies, and was happy at Marlborough. 'Let's hope that this war will be over before he is old enough to take part.' She told him too about Rose Cottage and brought him up to date with general family news.

But replying to Robin's letter, Binnie found, was far from easy. Things she longed to say to him she was unable to, and things she longed to hear from him she could not ask for.

A love letter was what she so wanted to write. *If only I could tell him what he means to me!* she thought. *At least I can write the word – everyone does, don't they?* And she ended:

'With love from Binnie.'

I wish I could put kisses with it, she thought.
  She didn't.

21

George and Henrietta Bone had brought up their children in the Christian faith. You went to church every Sunday and you said your prayers every day, morning and evening.

Binnie's prayers were, like most people's, essentially selfish: 'Please, God, look after ...' and then a list of loved ones.

Now especially, when two of those loved ones

might well be in mortal danger, she prayed earnestly and often.

True, she sometimes could not help thinking that families everywhere were praying to God to protect their sons, and yet so many of those sons' names appeared in the casualty lists. There seemed to be no guarantee that her prayers would be answered. Was it all just a matter of luck?

Ironically, the first casualty of 1916 – from among those that Binnie loved – was not Alec, now fighting in the trenches, nor Robin as he ministered to the Somerset Yeomanry, but Charles – Charles whom Binnie had supposed to be reasonably safe on his Lincolnshire airfield.

One morning the postman called at Combe Brindle House, bringing a letter from the Commandant of the Royal Flying Corps' Training Camp, a letter which Binnie read with horror.

Aircraftsman Bone, said the letter, had been involved in an accident resulting in injuries to his left arm so severe as to necessitate amputation.

He had, in the course of his duties, been swinging the propeller of a biplane to start its engine, and somehow – Binnie could not understand the technicalities – the motor had fired and then stalled, and as Charles had grasped the propeller blade to swing it again, the engine had re-started. Before he could get out of the way, the propeller had smashed his left arm. So badly was it damaged that the surgeons at the hospital to which he had been rushed had no option but to remove the whole limb.

Afterwards, Binnie could never quite remember how she had contrived to get herself to Charles's bedside, but get there she did as quickly as was possible.

Hoppy was left in charge at the house, with Granny Bone and Watty to call on if needed. Grandpa Reggie sent Toghill with the Silver Ghost to take Binnie to Bath railway station, and then there was a long series of train journeys, first to London and then, with several changes, to the Lincolnshire hospital.

What she always remembered quite clearly was walking into the ward and being unable, at first, to pick out her brother from among the men who lay in a dozen or so beds. But then she realized that all of them, as far as she could

see, had two arms, save the figure that lay, seemingly asleep, on his right side, his left shoulder
cocooned in bandages.

Charles, the Ward Sister told her, was heavily
sedated to combat the pain, but his general
condition was stable.

'He's young and he's strong,' the sister said,
'and he'll pull through all right, no doubt of that,
but of course he will be invalided out of the
service. Such bad luck! They tell me he wanted to
be a pilot.'

For half an hour or so Binnie sat at her
brother's bedside, watching his pale face, listening
to his heavy breathing. Then Charles's eyelids
flickered and he opened his eyes and saw her and
managed a sort of smile.

'Hello, Bin,' he whispered.

Binnie took his right hand and kissed it.

'I've lost a wing,' Charles said.

'Yes, I know, Charlie.'

'No flying for me.'

'No,' said Binnie.

'And no more cricket either.'

'Try not to worry about it,' Binnie said. 'Just

142

concentrate on getting better and stronger and we'll soon have you out of here and back home again.'

'Ah well,' Charles said, 'I can always take up tennis.'

When at last Binnie reached home again, it was to find two letters awaiting her, one from Lance-Corporal Bone and one from the Reverend Robin Seymour.

Alec's was, as usual, determinedly cheerful, as though he were enjoying this adventure in France. His only mention of soldiering was to say that his new non-commissioned rank might possibly be of only short duration. His commanding officer had recommended that he apply for a commission.

'If that happens', he wrote, 'I'll be back home before long, first as an officer cadet, and then if all goes well you will have the undoubted honour of being the sister of Second Lieutenant Bone. The General would have been pleased, I suppose.'

Robin mentioned little of his duties as a chaplain in the front line, save to say that, at the services he took, it had come as no surprise to him to find that the troops' favourite hymn was 'On-ward, Christian Soldiers'. He made no mention of the things which Binnie imagined he must be doing – comforting the wounded, giving the last rites to the dying, writing to bereaved wives or sweethearts or parents. Rather, his letter was a long catalogue of enquiries: Was she well? Were the rest of the family in good health? How were things in the parish? Was the elderly vicar man-aging all right? Were services in St Margaret's well attended? Was the Vicarage garden being properly looked after?

'What a string of questions!' he wrote. 'One last one – what chance of Charles being selected to train as a pilot? We need someone to take on von Richthofen, the German air ace. Charles had such a good eye when facing fast bowling that I can just see him shooting down the Red Baron, as they call him.'

This time he ended:

> 'Much love,
>   Robin.'

How much? Binnie thought. *I wish I knew.*

22

At the end of April 1916 Charles was invalided out of the Royal Flying Corps and came back to Combe Brindle House.

'Just in time for the start of the cricket season,' he said with a wry smile.

Most of the Combe Brindle village team had gone to fight for King and Country, but there were still older men keen to keep things going, and Binnie had a word with a retired major who was now the skipper. Thus Charles found himself once again on the pretty tree-girdled cricket ground behind the village pub, sometimes as an umpire, sometimes as scorer.

For Binnie, the most nerve-racking moment of each day was the arrival of the postman, in case he bought one of those dreaded telegrams from the War Office . . .

Coming through the flap into the wire letter-box on the inside of Combe Brindle House's front door might be ordinary letters, or bills, or, with luck, news from Alec or Robin.

But please, God, thought Binnie every day as she hurried to sift through the mail, *not one of those telegrams!*

In early May, one did come.

Binnie knew what it was. She also knew that such news – of capture, of wounds, of death – came only to the next of kin. She was next of kin to Alec but not to Robin.

She went to her office and sat down at her desk, holding the buff envelope in one hand, in the other a paper-knife. All she knew at that instant

146

was that something bad, maybe something terrible, had happened to her eldest brother, and she prayed that whatever this telegram had to say, it would not be the worst.

She slit the envelope, unfolded the sheet of paper within, and read:

War Office.   London.

It is with great regret that I have to inform you as next of kin, that your brother, 2622809 L/Cpl. Bone. A., was killed in action on 6.5.16.

There were some other words and the signature of some high-ranking officer, but Binnie's tear-filled eyes could not read them.

For some time she sat, holding the telegram. She was numb with shock and unable to think clearly. How did he die? What killed him? Did he die instantly? Where would they bury him? Robin would know – he must, surely? He would write and tell her – soon, please, soon! An arm lost and now a life lost. What next for her loved ones?

At last Binnie managed to pull herself together,

and she went to the telephone booth in the hall and asked for Grandpa Reggie's number.

Having told him the news, she walked down to Rose Cottage and broke it to Granny Bone and Watty.

Next she told Charles, who took the news in silence, but pulled her towards him with his one arm and hugged her tightly.

Afterwards she found Dodie and Fifi in the shed, cleaning out the livestock, and she told them as gently as she could of Alec's death.

'We must be proud of him, always,' she said, and she put her arms round them both and the three of them stood close together for a while in silence.

Then Dodie said, 'Edward must be told!'

'I'm going to phone him now,' Binnie said.

'D'you think,' Fifi said, 'that Alec is at peace?'

'I'm quite quite sure he is,' replied Binnie.

'One of the rabbits died last week,' Fifi said. 'He looked ever so peaceful. Just as though he was having a nice sleep.'

*

Next morning when the postman came, he brought a letter for Binnie in the now well-known handwriting of the former Vicar of Combe Brindle. Binnie took it to her office and sat at her desk and prepared to slit open the envelope.

What would it say, this letter that must have been written after, and with reference to, Alec's death?

6.5.16.

My dearest Binnie,

By the time this reaches you, you will doubtless have heard officially. But in case you have not, I have to tell you that your dear brother Alec has been killed, early on this very morning. Only an hour ago I said prayers over the grave in which we have buried him, in a little cemetery behind the lines, a cemetery in which, alas, many others of his fellows lie.

I believe, as you surely will too, that he is gone to meet his Maker, and that, as it says in the Bible, 'Death hath no more dominion over him.' There was no suffering for him, as I understand that mercifully his end was as immediate as could be hoped for. He was on sentry duty in a front-line trench, and must, for whatever reason – perhaps on hearing a noise and suspecting a raid – have ventured to look over the parapet. A German sniper shot him through the head. Alec, his comrades told me, died instantly.

It breaks my heart to tell you this news, dear Binnie. There is no way to soften the blow. I am only glad that it was I who was privileged to perform the last offices for your brave brother. He was a good soldier.

Trusting as I do – and you, I am certain, also do – in God's mercy, I believe that there must be some purpose in Alec's sacrifice.

Be proud of him,

With love,

Robin.

23

The year 1916 was terrible, not only for the Bone family but for thousands of families throughout the length and breadth of Great Britain.

Field Marshal Haig, who had taken over command of the British Army, decided in his wisdom that one last enormous effort by the British, supported for the first time by tanks, would finally burst through the German lines and end the war.

So on 1 July began the Battle of the Somme, and on that first day alone there were 57,000 British casualties. By November 1916, when the attack was finally called off, 600,000 of Haig's men had died, and all that was won in all those months was a handful of villages.

Just before this terrible battle was to start, Binnie was sitting in her office, looking out across the croquet lawn. Hoops and posts were now in place on the well-mown grass, and two mallets and balls were flung down where Dodie and Fifi had just finished a game. She was thinking, as she often did, of Robin Seymour. Usually he wrote weekly to her but she had not heard from him for some time.

As she stared out she suddenly became aware of a figure nearing the far end of the sunlit lawn, a tall uniformed figure making its way between the white hoops towards the house.

Binnie leaped from her chair, ran out of her office into the next room and flung wide the French windows.

'Robin!' she cried, and she dashed to meet him, arms outstretched. 'Oh Robin, is it really you?'

For answer, he held her tightly to him and they hugged one another, as two old friends might hug. Then he put her a little away from him and looked so tenderly at her face and she at his. Then they kissed, as two sweethearts kiss.

'I love you, Binnie,' said he.

'And I love you too,' said she. 'Oh Robin, come and sit down here on this bench and tell me why are you here; what has happened? Have you been injured? Why did you not tell me you were coming home?'

'I did not know myself forty-eight hours ago,' Robin replied. 'I have been given leave, the first I've had since I went out to France, and no, I'm not hurt.'

He took her hand.

'I'm just unutterably happy to be here, to be with you, my darling girl, whom I have loved for so long now.'

'Oh Robin, if you only knew!' Binnie said. 'How long leave have you?'

'Two weeks.'

'Can you stay here, at Combe Brindle House?'

'I must go to see my family, but then I'll be

back. There's a room at the Vicarage for me.'

'There's a room here for you,' said Binnie decidedly.

They looked long into each other's eyes, smiling, and then Robin took her other hand as well, and said, 'Binnie, dearest, I don't feel that I can ask you now, but when this wretched war is over, will you marry me?'

'No,' said Binnie. 'I will not wait till the beastly war is over.'

'Do you mean . . .?'

'I mean that I will marry you as soon as I can, on this leave of yours if it's possible.'

Before anything else could be said, Fifi came running out on to the lawn, stopped, and stared at the man sitting very close to Binnie, recognized him as he stood up, and said 'Oh hello, it's you! I thought you were supposed to be in France.'

'I've been in France,' Robin said, 'but I'm home on leave.'

'And,' said Binnie, 'we are going to be married!'

'Married?' squeaked Fifi. 'You're going to marry the Vicar?'

'Yes.'

'Gosh!' cried Fifi. 'I must go and tell Dodie!' and she hurtled off.

'Now the whole village will know,' laughed Binnie.

Robin smiled.

'One way of calling the banns, I suppose,' he said.

Binnie sighed.

'If only Alec knew,' she said.

'Maybe he does.'

'You were telling the truth, weren't you? When you said he was killed instantly? I'm sure you sometimes have to say that when really people die lingering deaths, don't you?'

'Yes,' said Robin, 'but I was telling the truth about Alec.'

He picked up the two croquet mallets that lay on the grass and handed one to Binnie.

'Shall we play, Miss Bone?' he said.

'By all means, Mr Seymour,' Binnie replied, 'and I'll beat you hollow.'

Whether she would have done was not to be known, for before they could begin, Charles came out through the French windows, and Fifi came haring back, followed by Dodie who had stopped to telephone Rose Cottage with the news. Granny Bone in turn had contacted the Fea grandparents at Littledown Manor and then had hurried up with Nanny Watts. Then out of the house came a beaming Miss Hopkins, with the old cook not far behind here, while out of the upper windows two of the housemaids were waving. Even Whittle the gardener came down from his greenhouses to see what all the fuss was about on the croquet lawn.

Later, Toghill brought the Silver Ghost purring up the drive, and Grandpa Reggie and Granny Fea joined the throng of well-wishers, to embrace their granddaughter and to shake the hand of the man who had probably just escaped a beating at croquet.

'Many congratulations, Vicar!' Grandpa Reggie said. 'Though I suppose I should be calling you "Padre" now you're an Army chaplain.'

'Call him Robin, Grandpa,' Binnie said.

'I will, I will,' said Reggie Fea.

'Can I?' Fifi asked.

'Can you what?' said Binnie.

'Call him Robin.'

'Better ask him.'

'Can I?'

'I should be very unhappy if you didn't, Fifi,' was the reply. 'Though, of course, people do change their names. Your sister won't be Binnie Bone much longer. Soon she'll be Binnie Seymour.'

'Binnie Seymour,' said Fifi thoughtfully to the assembled company. 'It sounds nice, doesn't it?' and she did a handstand, something she had recently learned to do, and everybody clapped.

24

At Rose Cottage that evening, the talk between the two occupants was all of the day's dramatic news.

'You must be so delighted, Patience,' said one.

'Oh I am, Helen, I am!' replied the other. 'So must you be, who has known Binnie from her birth. And how delighted my dear George and his Henrietta would be, could they but know.'

'And so would the General, I'm sure.'

'Oh yes, of course. And he'd be pleased to see Robin in uniform.'

At Littledown Manor much the same happened, with Granny Fea fluttering on in her usual way.

'What a handsome couple they make, don't you think, Reggie? Both so tall – though, of course, he's taller than her – and both so good-looking. He is such a handsome sort of man, and as for our Binnie, she is almost a beauty, you could say, and she's dark-haired and he fair and only eleven years older – that's not much, is it?'

'Henrietta and George would have been delighted to have Robin as a son-in-law,' said Reggie Fea.

'Oh yes,' said his wife. 'He would have had to ask George for her hand, wouldn't he? Who will he ask now? You, I suppose.'

'I dare say,' replied Reggie.

In fact he had already thought of this. Before leaving Combe Brindle House that afternoon and out of hearing of the rest, he had said quietly,

'By the way, Robin, since Binnie's father is dead, as is her other grandfather, perhaps you will accept my approval of the match?'

'I most certainly will, sir,' said Robin Seymour.

'Just thought I'd save you asking. And incidentally, though the General would certainly have approved of your calling him "sir", I'd sooner you just used my Christian name.'

In the days that followed there was much to be done in a short while if the marriage was to take place before the end of Robin's leave.

There was no time for the banns to be properly called, but because it was wartime, because the bridegroom-to-be was a serving officer and perhaps because he was also an ordained priest, Robin's application to his bishop for a special marriage licence was granted. More, the Bishop offered to conduct the wedding service himself.

Binnie had a mass of things to organize: a wedding dress (her mother's), bridesmaids (her sisters) and their outfits, a best man (Robin's brother), to say nothing of a host of arrangements – Edward to be fetched from school, invitations to be hastily sent and announcements made, and of course the preparation of a wedding feast for the Bones, the Feas, the Seymours and as many as possible of their friends.

Somehow at last it seemed as though everything was going to be ready by the chosen date, 1 July.

That day dawned bright and clear and warm. No one could recall having ever seen the church so full, of flowers and indeed of people. Every pew was filled to see the eldest child of the late George and Henrietta Bone married to the man who had married so many other couples there and whom they still regarded as their Vicar.

Edward and a young Seymour were the ushers, the big and the little bridesmaid looked charming, the bride beautiful in white as she came down the aisle on the arm – the one arm – of her brother Charles, the groom handsome in uniform.

Mercifully no one had any idea that on that very day, when the Bishop joined Binnie Bone and Robin Seymour in holy matrimony in St Margaret's, Combe Brindle, there began in France the Battle of the Somme. By nightfall, when the Silver Ghost carried the happy couple away to the railway station, tens of thousands of British soldiers had lost their lives.

There were forty-eight hours of Robin's leave left, and he and Binnie spent them, on the shortest of honeymoons, in a little inn high on the Quantocks, walking the hills both days in the glorious weather of that early July, with all the birds and the rabbits and the red deer for company.

They saw no newspapers and so knew nothing of the great battle that was raging, but neither could for long forget that very soon Robin would be out in France again.

On the evening of their last day they were sitting side by side on a seat, by the lawn in front of the inn, as the sun was setting. The sky was a maze of colours, mostly shades of red.

'Red sky at night, shepherds' delight,' Binnie said, 'which is good, seeing that you are the shepherd of your flock, one might say.'

'Somersets,' said Robin. 'A rare breed of sheep.'

'But then,' Binnie asked, 'isn't there some Old

Testament quotation, something about "lambs to the slaughter"?'

'Jeremiah,' Robin said. 'Prophet of doom. Gloomy old bloke.'

He turned on the seat to face his new wife.

'Listen, my darling,' he said. 'You are going to need one thing above all others in the months, years maybe, ahead.'

'What is that one thing?' Binnie asked.

'Faith. Yes, I shall be in some danger again. Yes, many of those lambs will go to the slaughter. But you must believe, as I do, that with a little luck and a lot of the help of God, I may be spared to come back to you again.'

'Oh Robin, my love!' Binnie said. 'I'll pray for you.'

'Pray on, sweetheart,' Robin said. 'As I think I told you, I'm a firm believer in the power of prayer. Now come along, Mrs Seymour, it's time for supper.'

Why, thought Binnie as they walked hand in hand across the lawn in the sunlight, *do the words 'The Last Supper' come into my foolish mind?*

25

It was indeed the last supper of Robin's leave, for on the following afternoon Binnie was standing alone on the platform of Bath Station as the London-bound train disappeared from her view.

One last kiss as her husband leaned from the window, then the guard's whistle, the puffs of smoke from the funnel, the hiss of the pistons and the grate of wheel on rail as the locomotive began to pull away, and there was nothing left to do but to wave to one another till each was gone from sight.

Again, Binnie could not stop herself thinking, *That might be the last sight I ever have of my husband.*

But as the carnage of 1916 dragged on and the year turned, the Combe Brindle postman brought, each week, one of those longed-for letters, addressed no longer to 'Miss Bone' but now to 'Mrs R. Seymour' – letters that told her that Robin was in good health and, he always said, in good spirits.

In early April of 1917, the United States of America declared war upon Germany, and optimists were quick to say that this could not fail to shorten the war. Pessimists, however, were not slow to maintain that there was no way of breaking the stranglehold of trench warfare.

'There's a long way to go yet,' they said, and they were right.

In that same month, Field Marshall Haig took Vimy Ridge (with the loss of 132,000 men).

Between then and November came the third Battle of Ypres and then the taking of Passchendaele (245,000 British losses this time).

Not until September of 1918 was the Germany Army defeated and then at last, by October, Germany was suing for peace.

All this time – with the occasional leave of course – Robin Seymour served his country to the best of his ability, armed not with rifle and bayonet like the men of his regiment, but with faith and hope and charity as he preached to the living, and comforted the dying and the bereaved.

On 11 November 1918, Germany surrendered and signed the Armistice, and so ended a war that had cost the two sides over eight million lives, with a further twenty-one million wounded.

But with, in his own words, 'a little luck and a lot of the love of God', the Chaplain to the Somerset Yeomanry survived unscathed and was sent home and demobilized.

On the first Sunday of 1919, Robin preached once more in St Margaret's Church, Combe Brindle, as its Vicar.

Binnie, sitting with her brothers and sisters,

was remembering that dreadful day six years and nine months ago, when Watty had broken the news to her of the loss of her parents, and of that other dreadful day when word had come of Alec's death.

She looked along the pew.

At the far end sat Fifi, now nearly twelve. The old nicknames of the Afterthought or the Rabbit Keeper were largely forgotten, though in fact she now had the free run of the shed, for Dodie, sitting next to her, was nineteen and more interested in handsome young officers than hairy old guinea pigs.

Next to Dodie sat Edward, seventeen. His stated ambition, to no one's surprise, was, one day, to create a butterfly farm, and Binnie, seeing him staring upwards at the roof of the nave, was fairly certain that he was thinking not of Heaven but of the chances of there being any interesting moths clinging to the hammer beams.

Beside Edward was Charles, before long to celebrate his twenty-first birthday, the end of his empty left sleeve tucked neatly into his jacket pocket. *He is always cheerful*, thought Binnie, *never complains, enjoys his umpiring and his scorer's job in the cricket season. Why, one day last summer the village team was a man short, and out goes Charles to bat one-handed and scores a few runs, what's more. He's a very brave man.*

As, I'm sure, was my eldest brother, who should be sitting here next to me. If he could but know, he'd probably be vastly amused to be told that he was not sitting next to Binnie Bone but to the Vicar's wife. If we have a son, I'm sure Robin will let me call him Alec.

In the pew behind were sitting Grandpa Reggie and Granny Fea, who had come over specially, and Granny Bone and Nanny Watts and Miss Hopkins.

After the service, when all had gone back to their respective homes – to Combe Brindle House, to Rose Cottage, to Littledown Manor – and the last parishioner had shaken Robin's hand in welcome, Binnie waited in the porch while her husband, in his vestry, changed out of his robes. Then they walked together across the churchyard to the Vicarage, and sat down to Sunday lunch.

'Binnie, my love,' said Robin as he set about

carving the sirloin of beef. 'It must seem very strange to you, doesn't it?'

'What must?' Binnie asked. 'Having you back here with me, safe and sound? In peaceful Somerset instead of war-torn France? Of course it does, Robin darling.'

'I didn't mean that. I meant here in the Vicarage instead of in the house that's been your home all your life.'

'I've simply left one home,' said Binnie, 'and come to another, and not very far away either.'

She looked out of the dining-room window.

'I can see it, across the churchyard. I wonder if Edward's having a go at carving their beef – Charles can't manage it with only one arm. Perhaps Hoppy's doing it. It's strange to think that when Father and Mother ate what was to be their last Sunday lunch, had they but known it, there were six of us Bone children sitting round the table.'

Robin put her plate before her.

'The eldest of whom,' he said, 'looked after her orphaned brothers and sisters and brought them all up and managed the housekeeping and everything else so wonderfully well. You looked after them like a mother.'

He put a hand on her shoulder.

'Which you will be, one of these days, I hope,' he said. 'There were six of you. How about six little Seymours?'

'Sounds nice,' Binnie said, 'but I can't promise.'

Robin took his own plate and sat down, looking out at the churchyard.

'I remember seeing you through this window one day,' he said. 'It was not long after the sinking of the *Titanic*. It was May, I think, and you were wandering about in the churchyard, picking something or other.'

'Dandelions, I expect,' said Binnie, 'for Dodie's animals.'

'And I remember watching you and thinking how pretty you looked – you were wearing a white dress as I recall, with a blue sash, and a kind of straw bonnet, like a milkmaid's. You must have been nearly eighteen, I suppose.'

'And I suppose,' said Binnie, laughing, 'that

you said to yourself, "That's the girl I'm going to marry"!'

'Nothing so romantic, I'm afraid,' said Robin. 'I just thought, "Hmm. That must be Binnie Bone."'